HONORED

THE MOUNTAIN MAN'S BABIES

FRANKIE LOVE

JOIN FRANKIE LOVE'S
MAILING LIST
AND NEVER MISS A RELEASE!

Ohh … and for more fun, be sure to join
Frankie's Reader Group
on Facebook
for access to exclusive giveaways and contests!

Edited by Teresa Banschbach
Cover by Mayhem Cover Creations
Copyright © 2017 by Frankie Love

❀ Created with Vellum

CHAPTER 1

onor

I keep one hand on the wheel as I wipe my eyes unsuccessfully, my minivan barreling down the highway as I leave the only life I've ever known behind. Tears streak my cheeks, my heart races, and even though there are three crying babies in the backseat of the beat-up van, I've never felt so alone in my life.

Which isn't saying much, considering I'm a sister-wife.

People are always around. Always watching.

Always judging.

But no one sees me as I escape.

My flip phone—the one I bought at Wal-Mart last week—buzzes. As it rings, milk seeps from my engorged breasts. Having a twelve-week-old baby will do that to a woman, especially when her infant is screaming from his car seat.

I can't pull over to answer the phone or nurse Titus because I have to keep driving. I must keep driving and never

1

come back. With the windows down, the summer sun warms me up to the idea of a new forever. A forever I never considered for myself.

Freedom.

An hour later the babies are asleep and I pull over to fill the tank at a gas station. My stomach growls, but I don't know if it's from nerves or the fact I haven't eaten in hours. I grab forty dollars from my wallet, debating taking another five for caffeine, but I don't have that much to spare. Not now. The $112 I scrimped to save is for this escape, not to spend on frivolities. I packed peanut butter and jelly sandwiches and carrot sticks. I can have one of those while I drive.

I hand the cash to the cashier, my eyes on the van.

"You okay, sweetie?" she asks, pointing at the milk stains on my blouse. But I don't have time to be embarrassed. You can't afford to be when your children's lives are at stake.

"I'm fine," I say, eying the Snickers bars on the counter.

"Are you traveling alone?" she asks. I look up at her then, her gray hair clipped back, revealing pale blue eyes. I lower mine, not wanting to be noticed. Just wanting to get far away.

"Yeah, it's just my kids and me," I say softly, knowing I have no man to protect me, take care of me—here or anywhere. Knowing I've never had a real man in my life. The father of my children is nothing but a cheat.

She clucks her tongue, picking up the Snickers and handing it over. "Listen, mama, the chocolate's on me, and grab yourself a coffee on your way out, okay?"

My eyes fill with tears again. I need this more than she knows. I blink away the memory of leaving my sister-wives, without telling them I was going for good.

But I needed more... and not just for me. For my children. For my sons.

"Thank you," I manage, wiping my eyes with the cuff of my hand-sewn blouse. "I don't know why I'm crying."

"It's the hormones. I remember. It's been a long time, but you never forget." She smiles warmly, then wags her finger at me, telling me to get a coffee to-go. I do as she insists.

"Thank you," I tell her, with 16-ounce cup of steaming coffee in one hand, pushing open the door with the other.

"And remember to take care of yourself, honey," she says as I leave.

Pumping gas, I look at myself through the van window, seeing my sleeping babies all in a row, and I think that the cashier has no idea what my life has been like.

Taking care of myself has never been an option. I haven't slept a full night in years, but even through the haze of restless nights with a newborn cradled against my chest, I know that being a twenty-two-year-old with three children under three is not the reason I'm always tired.

I screw the gas cap on and slide open the van door, unbuckling Titus, and as I reach over him his one-year-old brother Thomas stirs. I kiss his forehead, willing him to stay asleep. His two-year-old brother, Timothy, opens his eyes. They meet mine.

"Shush, now, sleepy head," I whisper, brushing a tendril of his blond hair away from his sweaty forehead. His head falls back, giving in to the sleep his tiny body craves as if he knows how badly I need him to stay quiet.

With Titus in my arm, I sit in the driver's seat, pushing the seat back so I can nurse him. He latches onto my nipple, my swollen breast releasing milk, and my entire body seems to relax for the first time in weeks.

My babies are safe. I am sound. We can do this. We are doing this.

I reach for the phone, seeing the missed call was from

Harper. I press call back and listen to it ring, only once, before she's on the line.

"Honor? Are you okay? Is the plan still in place?"

My eyes scan the empty parking lot, knowing that Luke won't even notice I'm missing until tonight, when he looks around the supper table, at his other two wives, and realizes I'm not there. That three of his sons aren't either.

It's my sister-wives, Kind and True that I have to worry about. They think I've left to do the grocery shopping... but eventually, they will realize I haven't returned.

"Yes," I tell her, the only person I could think of calling when I got the courage to leave. After all, she was engaged to Luke four years ago, before he started a cult and everything changed. "I'm about ninety minutes away. It's still okay, isn't it... you haven't changed your mind?" I sniffle, my emotions bubbling up again.

"Of course, I haven't changed my mind. You're my cousin. Just focus on getting here." Then, softening her tone, she adds, "That's all you need to worry about now."

"Okay," I tell her. "I'll get back on the road. See you soon."

"I should have come and gotten you," Harper says.

"No. I needed to do this on my own. I needed to do this for my sons."

"You're being really brave," she adds her words a comfort I need more than she knows.

Not wanting to cry, I tell her good-bye. Not feeling very brave. I just feel desperate. Desperate for my life to be more than it is now.

I buckle Titus back in his seat, turn on the van, and put it in drive.

Taking a bite of my chocolate bar, I look back at the gas station, thinking of the attendant. How sweet she was with me.

She was right about needing to take care of myself.

4

And I know that getting away from Luke is the first step in the right direction.

It's the best way I take care of my children. Of me, too.

I needed to get them away from their father, away from his cult.

I needed to run away in order to start over.

CHAPTER 2

awk

I've made a lot of shitty decisions leading up to tonight, but damn, even as it was happening I knew it was an all-time low.

It wasn't the first time I'd been locked in the slammer. And not the first time I took the fall for my friends.

After hours of sitting on a hard bench in a holding cell, Officer Bailey tells me bail was posted.

My eyes narrow. I have friends, sure, but they're about as likely to get a bond to bust me out as winning the goddamned lottery.

"Lucky man," Officer Bailey says as I follow him to a desk where I sign out and get my shit. Not that there's much for me. This town is feeling much too small these days. Can't get a fucking drink without someone wanting to start something.

I run my hand through my hair, listening as the officer explains I have to show up for my hearing next week.

"You say it wasn't your fault, Hawk, but you're still gonna need to stand before a judge," he tells me. Under his breath, he adds, so only I can hear, "And you need to find some new friends, son."

He can call me that because he and my ma used to date, years ago, when I was a teenager. My ma's been dead five years now, but I know Officer Bailey has a soft spot for me because of the past. Because of the memories... certainly not because of the woman my ma was when she died. A drunk who got behind the wheel.

"Finding new friends is easier said than done," I tell Bailey, shaking my head.

"I know you were trying to do the right thing by sticking up for your buddy, but you knocked the guy out cold; his wife's pressing charges," he says as if I don't already know it.

"I'm not trying to justify shit—"

Bailey cuts me off. "Yeah you are, and I understand why, but I'll keep seeing you in here if you don't change things for yourself, Hawk. You need to stop taking care of your friends and give them a chance to take care of themselves. It's time for you leave this place and start over."

"I got my job here," I tell him. "I can't just go."

He shakes his head and opens the door to the lobby. "Listen, it's not the tats or the muscles that are gonna get you in trouble."

I frown, not following.

"It's the way you are determined to stick up for the underdog that's gonna be the death of you. Besides," he adds, "you can't save them if you've lost yourself."

I clench my jaw at this, because even if it's fucking true, what difference does it make? Starting over is easier said than done.

In the lobby, I shake my head when I see my cousin Jaxon waiting for me, looking around, uncomfortable as fuck. He must be, he screwed around on Sheriff Martin's daughter; he's the reason he left town in the first place years ago.

Yet here he is. Bailing me out.

He's the only guy I know with as many tattoos as me, yet the two of us couldn't be more different. He got himself a wife and a bunch of mouths to feed and I don't envy him any of that.

Still, he's got his shit together.

I look back at Bailey, knowing he must have called him in.

Bailey just shrugs, gives me a small smile. "I can't help but look out for you." Before I can say anything, he goes back into the office.

"You came down here, for me?" I ask, hating that Jaxon left his home in the mountains, about ninety minutes from here, to get me out of jail.

"You're the closest thing I have to a brother, dumbass."

Jaxon's in his thirties, but I'm twenty-five. Growing up, he was always like an older brother to me.

I scratch my head, knowing I've fucked things up and hating that he's here, cleaning up after me.

"We should go to your place," Jaxon says as we leave the station. "You need to say goodbye to this town and get your shit."

I scowl, climbing into his truck. "And where do you think I'm going?" I ask as Jax pulls out of the parking lot.

"I think you're coming home with me. I'll give you work, the mountains are a fine-ass place to clear your head. What the fuck, Hawk? Starting fights?"

I push back. "I didn't start shit. I just finished it."

Jax gives me a sidelong glance, not having any of it. "You just happened to be in a bar fight, after getting arrested a few months ago for stealing a goddamned car—but you're clean as a fucking whistle?"

I shake my head. "You don't know shit, Jaxon," I tell him.

"You wanna explain it to me?"

I run my hand over my beard, not interested in Jaxon being some tough-ass guy to me as if he's my fucking father. I never had a father and I sure as hell am not looking for one now.

"You wouldn't understand, Jaxon. We're not the same, never have been."

Jaxon doesn't answer, and part of me resents the way he's changed as he's gotten older. Less a friend and more of a judge.

He turns into the bar parking lot where my truck has been since the bar fight. A sweet-ass '47 Ford pickup truck, glossy black with wooden rails. This is my motherfucking baby and I need to get her home.

Before I get out of his car, Jaxon tells me what he thinks. "I love you man, I do, but a year ago you were charged with breaking and entering. Your rap sheet is getting pretty fucking long. You're on a path going nowhere, fast."

I open the door, pissed that he thinks he has any fucking clue. I got that B&E charge because I was trying to get my friend Jim's tools after his ex kicked him out of the house. And this bar fight is the same fucking story—Trevor was getting harassed for no good reason.

Dammit. I slam the door shut, and Jax follows me to my truck.

"Why do you want me to come to the mountains, anyway?"

"We need another guy on our crew. I know you love the shop—but we both know you're not getting the hours you want."

"Being under the hood of a car is where I belong, not swinging a goddamned axe."

Jaxon shrugs. "There could be worse things than learning a new skill."

"I've saved up a shit ton of money over the last few years, I can ride it out until the shop starts getting more work. I plan on opening a shop of my own soon as I can."

Jaxon shakes his head. "It's great you've saved so much, but you'd be a fool to open a place here. Not in a town that can't even support one mechanic shop."

I grip Jaxon's shoulder, knowing the truth in that. Refusing to admit it to myself. And sure as hell not wanting to just randomly look on a map and choose a place to relocate. Deep down, I know I want direction, meaning. Some fucking purpose to my life.

Maybe this is the wake-up call I've been waiting for.

"You're right," I tell him, shaking my head. "But dammit, the mountains? What the fuck is there to do out there?"

"Spend time with your second cousins, chill out. At least out there, you won't blow through your cash."

I shrug, not knowing what I'm fighting so hard against. I've been meaning to come out to his place for ages, and after bailing me out tonight, I owe him, big time. "I'll come help your crew if you really need it," I tell him. "But if I'm working for you, I'm paying you back for helping with the bail. You understand that?" I look him in the eyes, meaning it. Right now, I'm accepting his offer, but I'm not taking any handouts.

"Understood," Jax says.

"But I need a week or so to finish up a car I've been working on for Trevor, but after that, I'll drive to your place, sound good?"

Jaxon frowns. "And so you can stand before the judge, right? I don't wanna lose that bail money."

"Right." I nod, not wanting to let him down. The last five years have been painful. It seems like I haven't been able to get a leg up since Ma died. It's always one thing after the next and I'd love to catch a real break.

"You promise you'll show? We're starting a new house next week, but we're still trying to wrap up the renovations on a little cabin -- that's where I'd send you. Buck is working on it and could use another set of hands."

"I'll be there."

"You're staying with me, okay?"

I cock a brow at him, trying to count in my head how many babies he's got in that place.

"The motel in town is seedy as shit—besides Harper will be pissed if you refuse our guest room."

I shake my head at this fool. "Damn, she's really got your balls in a vise, doesn't she?"

I think he's gonna push back on that, but instead, he grins like a lovesick puppy.

"Damn right she does, and I'm a lucky bastard because of it."

I laugh at him, knowing that I may learn to see what he sees in that mountain, but I sure as fuck am not going to see eye to eye on with him on having some woman rule my life.

CHAPTER 3

onor

Harper pulls me into a tight hug when I arrive.

"I'm just so glad you made it safely. It's getting kind of late."

"I got turned around on the main road. You really live in the middle of nowhere."

I take in my cousin—the unrepentant woman, as our family calls her. She's in skinny jeans and a loose cream-colored sweater, her toenails are painted lavender, her fingernails too. For a mother of five, she looks incredible. And it's not just the clothes... Harper looks happy.

"Well, I'm glad you made it OK. Let me get my shoes on and I'll help you with the babies."

She follows me outside, where I open the van door. I begin unbuckling my children and as Harper takes Titus from my hands, she tells me Jaxon will be home any minute.

I set Thomas on my hip and take Timothy's hand.

Walking back into the gorgeous custom cabin her husband made with his bare hands, she explains where Jaxon is. "His cousin, Ben, had some trouble tonight. He went into town to get him out of jail. Just left ten minutes ago. You probably crossed one another on the road."

"Trouble?"

Harper sighs as we walk inside. "Yep, he's hoping to convince him to stay here a while and work for us. He's a little rough around the edges... but then again, so is Jax."

Her kids are all at the dining room table eating supper, and she pulls out extra high chairs for my littles. "Wanna set Titus in the swing while we eat?" she asks, already strapping Timothy in a high chair.

I appreciate how child-proofed her house is, and I think how the house I just left is set up the same way. Between my sister-wives and I, we had eight children, all under four. Harper's large family doesn't intimidate me.

Placing Titus in the swing, I try to get my bearings. Harper is already pushing me toward the table and setting a bowl of potato soup in front of me.

"Eat. I bet you've been a nervous wreck all day." She laughs bitterly. "Well, longer than a day, probably. Gosh, I can't believe you went through with it."

"I had to," I say, sinking into the chair and looking lovingly at my children sitting on either side of me at the massive hand-carved table.

"Of course, you did, sweetie," Harper says, handing me a basket of rolls. "I just mean it was so brave of you."

I shake my head. "Not gonna be so brave when Luke realizes where I've come."

"When he finds your letter, he's going to be angry; livid—of course—but you gave him Jax's number, and I think that's going to be enough. He doesn't have much to stand on."

"I'm just worried he's gonna come after the babies." I rip a roll into pieces and hand them to Thomas, before dishing a small amount of my soup in a small plastic bowl for Timothy.

"He won't, though, and we both know that. He starts fighting you for them and he'll put his precious community at risk. He won't risk it."

Her words are meant to comfort, but they don't. They break my heart for my children. They will never know the love of a father. Looking around at Harper's children, a twinge of jealousy pierces me, knowing they'll never have the same struggle.

And that is if we can even manage to piece a life together for ourselves.

Right now, with my meager funds, I know we're going to need hand-outs for a long while.

I brush aside the tears and force myself to pick up my spoon. "I just have a lot to figure out."

Seeming to understand, Harper drops the topic and we focus on the kids—goodness knows there are plenty. We feed them, change them, put them in jammies, set up Pack 'n Plays for mine, and spend the next several hours settling them all in for the night. She has the kids and me in a spare bedroom downstairs, away from her family's rooms.

"You sure it's enough? I thought you'd have it to yourself, but then with Ben coming in, I figured we'd give him the only extra bed." Harper furrows her brow. "But he could always sleep on the couch."

"No," I tell her, looking at my babies all settled in for the night. "This is better. I want them close to me. Besides, I'm guessing this house gets moving at the crack of dawn, I'm sure Jax's cousin would prefer a bedroom with a door when the toddlers start banging around."

With the kids all down, we head back to the kitchen and I try to be useful by loading the dishwasher."

"Don't worry about that," Harper says. "I'm exhausted. Aren't you?" She sighs, grabbing a bottle of red wine from her kitchen island.

Harper smiles, pouring herself wine and offering some to me.

I raise my hand, motioning no.

"Oh, sorry. I forgot." Harper frowns. "It feels like ages since I left the family."

"Well, a lot changed," I say, adding soap to the dishwasher and starting the load. The last four years have been so confusing, starting with when Luke returned from Lord's Will Bible College ready to convert us to his belief system. My parents were on board, and so were Harper's. As an eighteen-year-old with no education, no money, and no way of leaving, I found myself promised to Luke, along with two other women who joined his church.

Polygamy was just one of his new convictions. We couldn't cut our hair, drink, swear, or question anything—or anyone. Especially him.

"I knew Luke was a dick before, but I never thought he would start a cult. And really, the polygamy shouldn't have surprised me as much as it did, he was always a cheat," Harper says, swirling her glass of red. "It's so sad, though, I haven't heard from James since he was forced out."

She leads us to the massive sectional in the great room. We sit down, her in her comfortable clothing, me in my long skirt and blouse—a clean one—and I try to feel at home. The truth is, my heart is still pounding from the exhilaration of the day. I feel so lost, so alone. What I want more than anything is someone to wrap their arms around me and tell me it's going to be okay. That I'm going to make it. I want to sink into the comfort of another person who has more figured out than I do.

Instead of voicing any of that, though, I say, "Luke kicking your brother, James, out was the tipping point for me. I'd look at my boys and wonder what would happen to them when they grow old enough to become competition. I wanted more for them."

We grew up religious... but Luke's cult isn't about believing in something bigger than yourself, about finding grace and unconditional love—no. Luke's cult has become something dangerous and has turned what was once a beautiful message of acceptance into something ruinous.

"Do you want me to call you Jenna?" Harper asks. "I wondered if Honor only holds bad memories?"

I bite my bottom lip, having already considered this. "No, Jenna is the name with bad memories. I can't go back to being her. Jenna was weak, and I don't want to be that girl anymore."

"But you were so young when Luke took you, it wasn't weak."

"Maybe that's true, but I like being Honor. It gives me something to strive toward. I want to be honorable, to be noble for my sons. I don't know how Kind and True feel about their names, but I know how I feel about mine."

Harper watches me closely, as if she has a lot more she wants to say.

"Just come out with it," I tell her. "Honestly, what are you thinking?"

Harper shrugs. "I'm thinking it's crazy to keep a name that Luke gave you."

Maybe Harper will never understand what the last few years have been like. On the outside I'm sure she thinks all of it was bad -- but that wasn't the case.

"If I hadn't gone through the last few years I wouldn't have my boys. They are my world. My everything. I wouldn't change my story if it meant I wouldn't have them."

"As a mother, I understand that in theory ... but aren't you at least a little bitter?"

I twist my lips and then shake my head. "I don't have space in my heart for anger. I'm just grateful to have had the strength to leave."

"You were always way more mature than me," Harper says smiling wistfully. "Even when we were kids-- you never got caught up in petty drama. You've always known who you are."

I raise an eyebrow, not seeing myself that way at all. I sure got caught up in Luke's cult for longer than I'd like to admit.

Just then the front door slams and I jump, startled. Harper's wine sloshes from the rim of her glass, and I apologize.

"Sorry, I just... I got..." I reach for a burp cloth on the coffee table, soaking up the wine, but Harper doesn't seem to care in the slightest. She's bounding across the room toward Jaxon.

"Is he here? Is everything okay? Was the drive rough?" She bombards him with questions. I watch Jaxon shake his head slowly at his woman, wrapping an arm around her. "You were supposed to call me on your way home."

"Damn, woman, everything's fine. And I did call, you just never answered your phone."

Harper twists her lips, and I realize I haven't seen her look at a phone all night.

She shrugs, gives a little laugh. "Oh. Well. I'm glad you're safe. But where's Ben?"

"He'll be here in a week. He must see the judge and wrap up some stuff in town. But he'll be here soon enough, thank God for that."

He kisses her then, not noticing me a few yards away. Or maybe he does and just doesn't care. I can't imagine what it

17

would be like to have a man like that, so utterly devoted to me.

I stand awkwardly, watching the pair, my heart aching for their familiarity, their playfulness—their complete love.

Jaxon walks over and gives me a hug too. "Glad you made it, Honor. You're safe now."

I exhale, wanting so badly to believe him. Needing to believe him.

Smiling, I tell them goodnight, thinking these two need some time alone.

In the bedroom, I lean over the Pack 'n Plays, kissing the heads of Timothy and Thomas. Then I reach for Titus and carry him to the queen-sized bed. Slipping under the covers, still dressed but exhausted, I pull Titus to me, holding him close to my chest, so grateful I have my children beside me. Breathing in his sweet baby smell, I will my eyes to close.

As I try to fall asleep, I imagine a man loving me the way Jaxon loves Harper—so completely.

It seems like a gift I'll never receive. But I have my babies, and I'm far away from Luke, and for now that is more than enough.

 onor

"Just go," Harper tells me. "You haven't left the house all week. Go get yourself a cup of coffee and slice of pie at Rosie's diner. We can manage the kids."

I look around Harper's living room. It looks like a daycare threw up. Harper's best friends, Rosie and Stella, were over all day with their kids. While it was nice to spend more time with Harper's girlfriends, I felt myself withdraw more and more as the afternoon passed.

I miss my sister-wives. Not in a way that would make sense to anyone else... not because they are friendly—no; they are quick to judge, sneer, and raise an eyebrow —but they are the only family I know.

Listening to Rosie moan about her husband Buck's dirty clothes on the bedroom floor or Stella telling us how her man Wilder is on diaper duty every day between seven p.m. and midnight, makes me think how I left my family. And sure, Harper and Jaxon are family... but they also have each other. Me? I have to figure out how to make a life for myself.

"I should stay and clean up," I tell her. The debris from a family dinner is all over the place. There are so many food crumbs on the floor that even Jaxon's dog, Jameson, can't eat them all.

"No way," Jaxon says, walking in with a fussing toddler in his arms. Cedar is flat out refusing to toilet train and has insisted on throwing a fit every time it's mentioned. Precious little lamb.

(Said no parent ever.)

"Seriously," Jaxon continues. "Luke is all talk right now. He's angry, but I can tell he won't come around here. You can have peace of mind over that."

Luke has been calling Jaxon almost daily, shouting at him, all the while condemning me. Jax isn't having any of it. Last night, he told Luke that he has no problem filing a restraining order himself if Luke is gonna keep harassing him.

"You sure?" I ask, wanting a little time to myself desperately. The picture of sitting down with a plate of pie I won't have to share with my kids is already forming in my mind.

Whipped cream. Cherries. Hot coffee. Flaky crust.

That self-care that the gas station attendant was talking about.

"We're sure," Harper says, taking Cedar from her husband's arms. With him on her hip, she tells him he'll get an M&M if he uses the potty like a big boy. "Go," she says, shooing me away and carrying her boy down the hall to the bathroom. "And find something of mine to wear, put on some lipstick, take down your hair. It will do wonders, promise."

I twist my lips together debating this as Jaxon turns on a

DVD for the gaggle of kids. Elmo starts babbling the ABCs and it's obvious he can take care of the crew.

Me? I need to go take care of myself.

—

An hour later I get out of my van at Rosie's diner. My long, wavy blond hair is loose around my shoulders, nearly to my waist, and the sundress I found in Harper's closet flutters at my knees as I walk to the restaurant. I feel free in the way I longed to a week ago when I left.

Free in the way I've longed for all my life.

Pulling open the diner doors I see Rosie isn't working. It's the new girl, Josie, the one I'd heard her talking about earlier today when she laughed about being the Rosie and Josie duo at the diner. She's beautiful, with a devil-may-care sparkle in her eye that Luke always warned against. Confident. Bright. Larger than life.

I press my pale pink lips together and feel foolish. She's all bright red lips, thick eyeliner, high heels—and totally confident.

I'm in flip-flops and lip gloss and feel at more risk than I ever have before.

But then she smiles at me, waves me in, tells me I look like a summer sunset: soft around the edges. Her compliments warm me to her instantly. Shallow, maybe, but my soul is parched for generosity, and she seems like a well, overflowing.

"Thanks," I tell her, taking a seat in a corner booth.

"What can I getcha?" she asks, pen and paper at the ready.

"Coffee. And pie."

"We got apple, peach, and cherry."

"Cherry. Please. And cream for my coffee."

"I'm on it." She turns away and I sink into the vinyl seat, relishing the late summer night alone.

She comes back over, pouring my coffee as the diner door swings open. In steps a man the likes of which I've never seen before. Apparently, neither has Josie because the mug she's filling overflows with steaming coffee.

"Dammit," she says, flustered by the man. "I'll clean that up, let me go grab a rag," she tells me, headed for the kitchen and leaving me alone in the dining area with a man who dominates the room. He's in a white t-shirt, arms covered in tattoos, and his beard makes Jaxon's look like a teenage boy's. His eyes are smoky gray and they land on mine.

I bite my bottom lip, press my thighs together, and manage to contain my whimper.

This man is more than handsome... he makes my body melt into the booth. I can't think of a time my body responded like this to a man... certainly never with Luke. Luke could press himself inside me and all it felt like was a clammy exchange I never wanted.

But one look at this man and my body reacts in a way I never considered before.

Full of desire.

A lifetime of pent up desire.

Josie comes in and wipes up the table, and I'd think this man would start checking her out as she bends at the waist, her tight jeans showing off her rear, her top low cut and revealing a set of breasts I'm guessing no baby has ever suckled. She looks like sex I've only ever dreamed about.

But when I look at him, I realize his eyes haven't moved off me.

"How can I help ya?" she asks once she's cleaned up the mess.

22

"I'd like a cup of coffee. A piece of pie."

She smiles. "That's what everyone's having tonight. Decaf or regular?"

He looks at me like we're finishing a conversation we never started.

"Regular," I tell him, not even knowing why. "And cherry. Cherry pie."

"Perfect," he tells Josie. "I'll have the same."

Josie cocks her eyebrow between us as he walks over to my booth as if trying to understand what's happening here.

I'm trying to understand, myself.

But I don't tell him no. I don't resist. In fact, I find myself sitting up straighter, looking him in the eye, wanting him to lead the way.

Tonight, I wanted to be free... but in a flash, all I want to do is follow.

Follow my heart... or at least follow the space between my legs. The space that is hot and bothered and wanting something it's never had before.

A real man.

"This seat taken?" he asks, already sliding in across from me.

I shake my head.

"I'm Hawk," he tells me, reaching a hand over the table.

"I'm Honor," I answer, taking his hand in mine. When we touch it's electric and I know people say there's no such thing as love at first sight but whatever this is... it's more than a handshake.

It feels like he's reaching over and not just offering me water from his proverbial well like Josie had—no. Hawk reaches over and pulls me in.

I let him.

awk

She holds onto my hand and I pray she'll never let go.

The last thing I expected to find when I finally showed up here at the base of the mountain where Jax lives was a woman like her.

She doesn't match this mountain vibe. She's not rugged like she was born here, or jaded like she left the city but keeps looking back—like the waitress.

No, this woman across from me, with her hand in mine, looks like she blew in from a world I've never been to. A world where a greasy mechanic sure as hell wouldn't belong. She's soft brush strokes to my steel engine but for some reason, I can't seem to let go.

She runs her thumb over the callouses on my palm and her fingers are like pinpricks of pleasure, hinting that they know the right places to touch to make a grown man cave.

Hell, she's given me nothing but her name and already I'm

willing to give her the whole damn world. She may be sitting in a booth, but I can see her curves, her full breasts, and immediately know she's the most beautiful woman I've ever seen.

"Honor? Nice name, it's different," I say, picking up my fork and taking a bite of the pie the waitress has dropped off.

"Thanks," she says. "So is Hawk." She takes a bite of her pie. There's whipped cream on her fork and I swear to God it gets me hard as fuck just thinking about her mouth being filled with that sweet cream.

She smiles at me, but the smile doesn't quite reach her eyes. And when I look in them, I see pale blue pools of water; there's a depth to them. Eyes I could swim in.

Eyes that tell me she's been through hell and back, but she hasn't drowned.

I understand that. After my ma died—killing the other driver in her recklessness—I was torn up inside. My ma's choices ended the life of another. It was paralyzing, realizing that it can all end in an instant.

In theory, I wanted that realization to propel me into being a better man, but in fact, all I've been is the vigilante for my friends' justice. Picking fights they could have owned themselves. Fighting, but not for the things that matter.

One look at Honor and I want to fight for her in ways I don't even understand.

I want to protect this woman who looks like she's seen better days.

"You come here often?" I ask, not even cringing at my line because I swear to God, I had no good reason to stop at this diner on my way to my cousin's place—but I couldn't help myself. I was drawn here. Craving something I couldn't even put my finger on.

At least not until I saw her.

Now I know exactly what I wanted.

Want.

Her.

"It's my first time," she says, picking up her coffee.

"Just driving through?" I ask.

She shakes her head. "No, I'll be here a bit."

I nod, the idea of staying around this mountain suddenly not seeming so bad.

"Me, too."

She smiles then, her cheeks turning pink and I realize that I am having the same reaction on her as she's having on me.

"Does it feel like..." I start but she cuts me off.

"Like we've met? Or at least... know one another?"

"Yeah," I say slowly, looking at her with more discernment. "But I know we haven't met before. I'm sure of it."

"Oh yeah?"

I grin. "There's no way in hell I'd forget you."

She laughs, soft and sweet like a cherry blossom in bloom. The summer wind blowing her delicate fragrance over my hardened heart. Instantly, I've softened to her, and by the way she licks her lips and sighs with longing, I know she's a flower ready to bloom.

I may not have all my shit together—but I can certainly help part her petals and show her how a garden grows.

"So, what is a pretty thing like you doing at a diner all alone?" I ask, hating the stupid line, but also needing to know. Needing to know her.

She offers me an innocent shrug. "I needed a night off, I guess. Life can be hard, ya know? Really stressful?"

I nod, my jaw tensing, hating that this woman's life is ever hard. Looking down at her cherry pie I smile. "So, you're telling me you're a stress eater?"

She laughs at that, smiling like she needs more smiles in her life.

"You're beautiful when you laugh, you know that?"

She lifts the fork to her mouth. "I bet you use that line on all the girls."

I shake my head. "Naw, just the ones I want to get to know better."

Her face flushes then, a rosy blush filling her cheeks.

"Am I embarrassing you? Coming on too strong?"

She squares her shoulders then, lifting her chin as if made of more determination than I pegged her for. And even though she looks like a wildflower, a woman used to growing wherever she can manage, she's rooted in something. She knows who she is.

I want to know her too.

"I'm not embarrassed." She twists her lips, as if trying to conceal a smile. "Honestly, I like it. It feels good to hear a compliment like that, even if I'm not the only girl you say that to."

"I'm not bullshitting you, Honor. You *are* beautiful."

She wipes her mouth with her napkin, then presses her lips together, a smile peeking out. "Thank you."

I take her hand in mine, lacing my fingers with hers. "You're welcome."

We stare at one another for a beat too long. Or a beat just long enough. A beat to know this night has just begun.

"You wanna get out of here?" I ask, pulling out my wallet and throwing a twenty on the table.

I don't wait for her to answer because this girl is already on her feet.

She was ready to go before I ever sat down.

Is this what love at first fucking sight is? Because damn, I swear I've spent my life in the dark and am suddenly blinded by the truth. The truth of her. Us.

I can't look away, even if I wanted to.

But I don't.

I want to see her for what she is.

And tonight, she is mine.

—

In the parking lot, I point to my truck. "Wanna go for a ride?"

She nods, then hesitates, the first time I've seen her take a second guess about this. About me.

"How about we just drive down to the bluff a mile down the road? There's a nice lookout I saw when I was driving through."

She nods again but her eyes flit around the parking lot and I try to follow her gaze. "I can't be long. Just an hour. Okay?"

I smile at her, the setting sun framing her face like she's been sent from heaven just for me. Glowing and pure and a sweet fucking dream. "Anything you want, angel."

She shakes her head as if she's embarrassed. For a second, I think I've gone too far with my words, but as I open the door to my truck for her, and she glides onto the bench seat, she looks up at me with those pale blue eyes and they tell me she isn't embarrassed at all.

She's relishing this.

Wordlessly, we drive to the bluff, the parking lot empty, and I'm about to put the truck in park when she shakes her head. "No," she tells me. "Down there."

She points to another parking spot, nestled in the trees, more discreet.

I look over at her, my cock a fucking rock at this point, and damn, I wasn't thinking I'd take this innocent angel so soon; thought she'd want to take her time, get to know me, but she insists.

"Please Hawk, down there, where it's more... private."

I give her a sidelong glance, loving the way she so easily tells me what she wants.

"You don't need to tell me twice," I tell her, putting the truck in reverse and driving to the spot tucked away, far from anyone who may be driving past, line of sight.

I park the truck then, with the setting sun in front of us and the mountain range behind us. The only thing right here, right now, is us.

"You always this sure of what you want?" I ask as she unbuckles and turns to face me.

"Not always," she says almost too faint to hear.

"But now?" I ask, reaching for her, cupping her cheek in my hand, not wanting to take away this angel's innocence before she is ready. She looks like a virgin; untouched and pure. "Now you know?"

"I know what I want, Hawk. For the first time in my life, it's all beginning to make sense."

Her words don't scare me—and hell, in the past they sure as fuck would have had me running from a girl who spoke with such clarity.

But not now. Not Honor.

Her words are a balm to my restless soul, effortlessly easing me into the idea of being a different sort of man.

I kiss her then, partly because I want to. But mostly because I need to. And I know she needs it too. Needs me.

I kiss her. And don't stop there.

CHAPTER 6

onor

His lips touch mine and my heart beats fast, my body hot and willing.

I may be a sister-wife, and have a man who calls himself my husband—but I'm not married. Polygamy is illegal, and Luke had already married True when I was forced into the church—the one he formed—and sealed to him as his wife.

I laid with him, had children with him, but he has never once been my partner... my lover. My spouse. He is the man I lived with and the man I ran from. But legally, we are not bound by anything beyond our flesh and blood.

Certainly, not bound by the bonds of holy matrimony.

Which is why when Hawk kisses me, I kiss him back.

"Your lips are like honey," he tells me, pulling back and looking into my eyes. His words are so sugary, not at all matching the way he appears on the surface. Hardened and tough. "So damn sweet."

I shake my head. "Kiss me again," I tell him, my body already demanding more.

He does, his lips press against mine, and my mouth parts, inviting him in. His tongue finds mine, and my skin pricks with pleasure. His hands run down my back, pulling me closer to him, and I sink into his hold.

My dress is short and as I lean toward him, it inches up past my thighs. I've never been so exposed, but with Hawk, it feels right. The moment I saw him I felt safe and seen.

I felt like for the first time in forever, I was in the right place at the right time.

So, I'm taking this moment without looking ahead because I don't know what the future will hold. My babies will need me and I'll need to be strong every day.

Which is why right now I'm going to let myself be weak at the knees.

I'm going to let myself be his.

"Oh, angel," he whispers, kissing my ear, my neck, my nose. "You are fucking unreal." His hands run over my butt, over my exposed leg. "I want you so badly."

"Good," I tell him, breathing in his rugged scent of gasoline and fresh air and leather. He smells like a man who knows what to do with me. "Because I want you, too."

He pulls me to him like I don't weigh a thing and I straddle him, feeling his hardness beneath me. I close my eyes, savoring this sensation. A man wanting me so desperately. Not using me today and his other "wife" tomorrow, his next "wife" the day after that. No. Hawk isn't asking for anything other than what this moment can offer us both.

His hands rest on my butt, he licks his lips. "You sure, baby? If it's your first time..."

I shake my head. I may be inexperienced in many things... but I am not a virgin. I am a mother of three.

I love my children more than life itself and will be fiercely loyal to them until the day I die—but Luke took things from me I can never get back. And when I look at Hawk, a man I've known less than one hour, who holds me like he won't let me go... it's like he found me at the exact right moment. The moment I needed him.

"It's not my first time," I tell him. "But I wish it were."

He exhales, and I think the idea of taking my virginity was a hold up for him. But then his eyes darken, the smoky gray turns nearly black.

"Did someone hurt you?" he asks.

"Before. Yes."

His hold on me tightens protectively. "I'll fucking kill them."

I shake my head. "Tonight, I don't want to think about the past... or the future. I just want to be here. With you."

Hawk pulls me to him, wrapping his arms around me, and kissing the top of my head. I feel tears well up in my eyes and I let my face nuzzle in his chest. There is something magical happening here... I just met this man, yet he's cradling me in his arms like he was made to take care of me. And deep in the cracks of my broken heart, I want him to.

"Let me make love to you." he says, drawing my face back to his with the crook of his finger. "Let me make the wrongs right."

He opens the door of the truck, and he carries me out of the cab. He lays down a blanket in the bed, and I won't ask why he has one at the ready. It doesn't matter... just like all the things I'm keeping back don't matter either. Not right now. Right now, all that matters is this.

Us. Taking what is ours.

Standing in the bed of the truck, he offers me his hand. The sun has set, and in the darkness, no one can see the two of us. No one sees as he helps me up, as we stand before one another, our bodies pulsing with desire.

No one sees as he tells me to lift my arms to the sky, as he lifts the hem of my dress and pulls it over my head. My hands instinctively cover my belly. Stretch marks streak it, but in the dark, he can't see them, so I let him move them away. I let him run his hands over my bare skin, and when he unbuckles his pants, steps out of them, and pulls his white t-shirt over his head, my hands know where they belong.

Running over the ladder of muscles on his abdomen, his skin hot and sweaty, he pulls me to him, hard. As if our exposed bodies need to be covered by one another.

He cups my face in his hand, kissing me, this time with a fierceness I hadn't felt in the cab. As if his masculine potency has been unleashed, standing under the moon with a near-naked woman in his arms. I whimper beneath him, wanting more, wanting it all.

"Lie down, angel," he tells me. "I need to touch you."

I do as he asks, lying on the wool blanket, my eyes looking up at the stars. Making a wish.

I wish I may, I wish I might. Have this wish I wish tonight.

That this moment will stay in my memory for always. That it will never be taken from me. That I will always feel as I do now. Like I am enough.

"What is it?" he asks, his hands on the waistband of my panties, ready to pull them down and take all of me. "Don't cry, baby."

"They're not sad tears," I tell him, my throat dry and my chest heaving and just so utterly grateful to have a night where I feel like someone beautiful. I didn't know how badly I needed it.

"No more tears tonight." He leans down, his mouth inches

from mine. "But I am going to have you crying out pretty damn soon."

I laugh softly, never having been this close to a man who spoke with this level of authority.

"Promise?" I ask.

"It's a goddamned guarantee." Then Hawk slips off my panties, runs his hand between my thighs, and groans.

"What is it?" I ask, very aware of my body. "Is something wrong?"

"No, baby. You're just so fucking wet." His fingers press against me and I inhale sharply. He feels me, and groans again. Which causes me to smile. He wants this too. "I want you so badly."

"Then take me, now," I tell him, reaching under his boxers, feeling his hard, velvety length. My body reacts to feeling him, my core alive and sopping wet. I know his fingers are soaked as he strokes me gently, touching my folds with tender intention. "Make me cry out," I tell him. "Erase my bad memories and give me a new one."

"Oh, baby, I'll give you more than one good memory tonight. I plan on giving you several."

CHAPTER 7

awk

Her pussy is warm and ready, and my cock is fucking on fire.

"Fill me up," she begs after my fingers have fucked her nice and slow. This angel under me is a godsend and if I believed in signs I'd say I fucking found one. I debated this decision, coming here to work at Jaxon's request, wondering if I should have just stayed put and looked for more mechanic work—but after an hour on this mountain I know I'm right where I belong.

With Honor.

Now.

And fucking forever.

She doesn't know all that yet, but I plan on showing her. I'm not letting this innocent angel go. No way in hell. We're just getting started.

I roll on a condom, wishing I weren't, but I need to do

35

everything in my power to treat this woman like she deserves. With respect and integrity.

"I need you so badly," I tell her, easing myself inside of her. "I want to fill you up until your pussy explodes."

She giggles beneath me. "Your words are so dirty, Hawk," she says, wrapping her arms around my neck, looking into my eyes.

"You like it filthy, don't you?" My cock loves her narrow cunt, and I fill her up so fucking fast.

"I've never had a man speak like that to me... but it sounds good on your lips. But I think..." she says, moaning as my cock presses inside of her, "I think anything would sound good coming from you."

"I won't just talk dirty then," I tell her, running my hand over her large tits, still covered in a bra. "I'll talk filthy-sweet to you, how does that sound?" I pump inside of her, her legs wrapping around me, rocking with me. Her wet little pussy tight around my cock.

"That sounds good," she pants, her eyes closed as I fuck her under the dark sky and bright stars. She pants as I fuck her for the first time, swearing to a god I've never believed in that I won't do anything to fuck up this moment for Honor. Not now, not ever.

"Oh, Hawk," she moans, clawing at my back. "Don't stop."

"I'm not gonna stop, you pretty little angel; I'm gonna fuck you until your pussy whimpers; until you scream my name; until you're ruined for all other men."

She moans louder as I rock against her. I fill her up and she begs for more. I fuck her harder, imagining all the ways I am going to take her in the days and weeks and months to come.

On her back and against the wall. In the green grass and in the water. With her on her knees and my cock deep inside her. From behind, my hands on her luscious, creamy ass. I'll fuck her until we collapse, and I'll fuck her until we can't see straight.

But now I fill her up, looking down at her like the goddess she is, her long hair strewn out, her pale blue eyes locked on mine, and I want to be the best man in the world, I want to carry her in my arms and make a home for her and protect her from the beasts in the world who don't know what it means to take care of a woman.

"Oh, Hawk," she cries, coming hard, her body pushing against me as I hold her close, as I pound her perfect pussy until I come too.

Until I feel a rip, and the reality hits me.

"Fuck."

"What?" she manages as if trying to remember how to breathe. "What is it?"

"The condom," I tell her as I come in her, wincing at the realization of what's just happened. "I think it fucking broke."

Her eyes go soft.

"Are you on the pill?" I ask, brushing her hair from her eyes.

She shakes her head no, ever so softly. "But I think we're okay," she tells me.

"Fuck, you sure?"

"I know my cycle really well. I think we're okay."

I pull out of her, taking off the ripped condom. "In that case, let me fuck you again without that on."

She blushes so hard I can see it under the light of the moon. "You want to... have me again?"

"No, I want to fuck you again."

She nods. "Let's."

I roll beside her in the truck bed, and wrap my arm around her shoulders, she nestles against me. "I think we should get another condom first, Honor. The last thing I want to do is get you knocked up. You're way too young to be a mother."

At this, I feel her stiffen in my arms.

"What is it?" I ask.

"I should get home, actually." She sits up, suddenly in a hurry.

"Let me get dressed and I'll drive you back then."

"Thanks, Hawk." She smiles, slipping on her panties. "That was..."

"Fucking amazing," I fill in for her.

She laughs, pulling on her dress. "Yes, it most certainly was."

—

In the parking lot of Rosie's diner, I realize I'm starving. I didn't have dinner and only took a few bites of the pie.

"You wanna come in and get something to eat?" I ask. "I'm gonna go get a burger."

She shakes her head. "No, I really need to go."

"Well, I need your number first. Because, baby, this isn't the last you'll be seeing of me."

She blushes again, her feelings so completely revealed, and I love that. She isn't putting on a fucking show. She is exactly who she says she is.

"I don't actually know my number..."

"What?" I cock a brow at her. "How do you not know your phone number?"

"I got a phone last week and haven't memorized it."

"You trying to get rid of me?"

She laughs. "No. Not at all. It's just I honestly don't know. Hey, why don't you give me your number and I'll call you?"

I nod, find a scrap of paper in the glove box and she presents me a pen from her purse.

I write the digits and hand it to her. "You better call me or I'll be looking up and down this mountain for you. Understand?"

Smiling, she takes it. "Understood."

"You sure you'll be okay driving home alone?"

She looks at me like I'm crazy. "I know how to take care of myself," she says.

I nod, taking her hand and kissing it. "I believe you know how to do a lot of things, Honor."

"Oh, yeah?"

"Yeah. Like you knew how to steal my fucking heart."

She bites her bottom lip.

"You mean that, Hawk?"

I nod. "I never say things I don't mean."

She leans over, kisses me softly, a kiss that could be mistaken for a whisper. "Neither do I."

"So, if I tell you I've fallen for you in the space of one night, what would you say to that?" I ask.

She runs her hand over my beard, through my hair, touching me so tenderly that there is no denying she has the hands of a saint. She could fucking heal my hard edges with those hands.

"I'd say I am one very lucky woman." She kisses me again, then adds, "And I'd say my wish came true."

She gets out of the truck, then, not looking back and I watch her climb into a minivan, with rusted hubcaps and a crack down the front window. She drives away and all I can do is hope like hell she calls.

If not, I'll be combing this mountain for her.

onor

Harper and Jaxon want to know how my night went, and I thank them for giving me a few uninterrupted hours.

"Of course; we're family," Harper says. She and Jax are snuggled up on the couch with their youngest between them. The rest of the house is asleep.

"Speaking of family, it sounds like my cousin is gonna be here tonight. He texted me a few hours ago, saying he was coming into town a day earlier than we expected him."

"Is it rude if I don't stay up to greet him?" I ask, feeling exhausted. I'm craving alone time to think through what I did tonight.

"Not at all," Jax says. "You'll meet tomorrow."

"Okay, thanks," I say. "Goodnight then."

In my room, I check on the boys, all three of them are out cold, and I step into the Jack and Jill bathroom and lock the other door, connecting to the other guest room. I'm not sure when Jaxon's cousin will be getting in and I want to take a shower before I go to bed.

I turn on the hot water and slip off my clothes. I look at myself in the full-length mirror, my breasts feeling full since it's been a few hours since I've nursed Titus. I trace the places Hawk touched me, not feeling ashamed for sleeping with a stranger, letting a man I'd never known before fill me with himself.

My body has changed so much over the last three years, my boys all less than a year apart. I'm grateful Hawk saw me in the dark, when my less beautiful parts were hidden, I don't think I would have had the guts to strip to nothing in front of him with the lights on.

I step into the shower and wash away the night, but not the memory. No, that is tucked close to my heart, and not going anywhere.

In the morning, the first thing I hear is someone knocking. Not on my door, but on a different one. I jolt out of bed, not having slept so soundly in ages, but apparently, my body needed a massive orgasm in order to sleep through the night. Titus is in bed with me, still out cold, and Timothy and Thomas are sleeping too. It must be early.

I roll my arm out from under Titus, careful not to wake him, and tiptoe from the bed, pulling at my tank top as I walk to the noise in the bathroom.

I open my door and realize the knocking is from the other side of the bathroom door. You can only access the bathroom from the guest rooms and I realize I left that door locked last night.

And Jax's cousin is coming in.

I'm in a pair of leggings, and my breasts, while not in a bra, are at least covered.

"Sorry," I say. "I totally locked you out."

I open the door and just about fall on my face.

"What?" I sputter, looking at the man before me. "Uh, who, wha… uh? Hawk?"

He looks equally shocked.

"Honor?"

"Did you follow me home? Why are you? What is…"

He shakes his head. "I didn't follow you. Hell, let me get this straight." He pauses, running his hand down his beard as if trying to process seeing me here. I'm trying to process it too. "You're Harper's cousin?"

"Yes. And you are?"

"Benjamin Hawk."

"Ben. Cousin Ben. You are Jaxon's cousin?"

He nods, grinning now, and steps toward me. "I want to talk, I really do, but I gotta piss like a motherfucker."

I shake my head. "You can't talk like that; not here," I tell him.

He steps past me and pulls out the glorious cock I had inside of me the night before. I can't breathe.

"No," I hiss. "The kids."

He shrugs. "Harper and Jax have their kids upstairs with them. And the house is still asleep."

I shake my head, unable to get out a sentence.

"I thought it was too good to be true, that I met you last night. But it wasn't just in my head. This is destiny, Honor," he tells me, looking over his shoulder at me as he pees in the toilet.

How is this even my life?

"No," I wave my hands in the air. "It's not… it's complicated."

He pulls up his boxers, looking cocky and disheveled with his bed head, his shirtless chest, his tattoos more menacing in the light.

"Not that complicated. Just a few crazy kids shacking up at their cousins' place. Doesn't seem complicated, seems like fate."

I exhale, distraught. My high from last night fading fast as the reality of the day glares in my face.

I don't know what to say, but I don't have to say anything at all. Titus' cry says more than my words ever could.

"Shit, did we wake up Harper's babies?"

I laugh a little too sharply. Colder than I ever am. But also sad, realizing more than ever that whatever magic washed over Hawk and I last night is going to fade fast. I already made my choices. Three choices named Thomas, Timothy, and Titus.

"That's not Harper's babies," I tell him, stepping back in my room, the door opening wide enough for him to see the truth. "Those are my babies."

I know Hawk's eyes are on me as I take Titus from the bed and pull him into my arms, but I don't know what to say. I wasn't lying when I said it was complicated.

"You're a mother?" he asks, stepping into my room. A movement that surprises me, because honestly, I thought for sure he'd run away.

I nod, sitting on my bed, cradling my three-month-old in one arm, and pulling down my top, offering him my milk.

"A mother of three."

Hawk is in the middle of my room, in his boxers, and looks at Timothy, then Thomas in their respective Pack 'n Plays.

He swallows, and I swear he looks... choked up. Is that possible? "Are you a wife, too?" he asks, his jaw tight, his eyebrows in a firm line.

I shake my head. "Not exactly." I swallow. "But like I said... it's complicated."

"Want to try and untangle it?" he asks, sitting down beside me on the bed.

He doesn't walk away, he stays. Like he genuinely wants to find the ends of the string and thread them back through properly.

"You won't like my story."

He laughs softly. "You won't like mine, either."

Titus has fallen back to sleep, and I stand and set him in his crib, knowing with this last feeding he is going to sleep for another few hours.

"I'm gonna need some coffee to explain this."

Hawk looks around the baby-filled room. "I think I'm gonna need something stronger than that."

CHAPTER 9

awk

I follow Honor into the kitchen, where she's making coffee in a long bathrobe. It's fucking unreal that she is here and I am here. I need the whole story, now.

But more than that... was everything I thought last night... that she and I were destined to meet, that me being here, now, was fate—was it all a fucking joke?

She's a mother of three... and more than that... I need a clearer answer on whether she is married. I can't imagine a woman as sweet as her lying about something so big.

No. It's impossible. This woman is a treasure, mother or not—hell, wife or not. I still know she is meant to be mine.

"Hey, angel," I say, coming up behind her, kissing her neck.

She steps away from me, turns to look me in the eye. "Don't. You can't. I mean. Harper can't know that..."

I lean in close. "That I fucked you last night? That you cried out my name as I filled you up?"

She bites her lip, holding in a gasp. "Yes, that, exactly."

I reach behind her and grab my cup. "Where do they keep the whiskey?" I ask.

Before I get an answer, though, Jaxon bounds down the steps, eying me coolly. "You looking for whiskey your first day on my crew? No way in hell, asshat."

I raise a hand in defense, knowing if I just explained what I just learned this morning, he'd certainly understand. But Honor shakes her head with a fierceness I don't expect. Hissing she begs, "Don't. Please."

Jaxon doesn't hear, and when Honor hands him her cup of coffee he just says thanks, and as he lifts it to his lips he says, "So you two met, I take it?"

I nearly choke on my coffee, but I can't see Honor's face because she is already back at the coffee pot pouring some for herself, but her shoulders stiffen, and I hate that. What I really want to do is step behind her and rub her back; she is a mom with a newborn. If anyone needs a break it's her. I'm ashamed at how lax I've been the last few months. I should have worked harder at getting my shop set up. Made more of an effort to get my life in order so I would be ready for her to enter it.

Now, I feel like I'm a thousand steps behind.

"We met," I tell him, keeping it civil. But I'm unable to resist adding one comment. "You never told me Harper's cousin was so beautiful."

Jax reaches for a banana, and peeling it, he explains. "Well, Honor hasn't exactly been on the playing field."

I frown, looking over at her, but her eyes are on the ground. I need to know this angel's story, but I don't want to hear it from Jaxon.

"When do we head out for the day?" I ask.

"In fifteen minutes. I was actually coming down thinking I would have to come wake your sorry ass up, but here you are, up and at 'em."

Honor twists her lips, about to say something, but holds back.

"Why are you up so early, Honor?" Jax asks her. "Did Hawk wake up your kids?"

"No, Hawk didn't do anything wrong. Titus was crying earlier," she tells him. "I couldn't fall back asleep."

Jax nods. "I'm glad I caught you, actually. Last night after you went to bed I got some really messed up texts."

I see Honor melt at this words. And not in a good way. In a lost way.

"Luke?" she asks.

Jax nods. "He's getting really aggressive. I know you said you don't want a restraining order but I don't think he is happy with the story you gave him."

"I didn't lie. I told him I needed time away," she says, huffing. "And I do." Her eyes brim with tears, and I want to wrap her in my arms, but Jax is here, and she's clearly uncomfortable with him knowing about our night.

Jaxon shrugs. "Look, either you need to talk to him yourself or you need to involve the police."

She shakes her head, adamantly. "Not the police. It wouldn't be fair to the other wives. The children."

My eyes narrow at this. Other wives?

"He is still your husband," Jax says. "And the father of your children."

"He's not my husband, not by law. You know how awful he is—better than most." She shakes her head, tears were gone now, now she is just plain old angry. "I don't want to involve the police. If that is what you want to do, I'm going to go back home... it's too risky for the other people I love."

Jaxon sets down his coffee. "Look, I'm not trying to upset

47

you. Harper will be wringing my neck when she finds out I upset you. But look, Honor, you need a plan."

"Why?" she asks. "Are you kicking me out?"

Jaxon rolls his eyes. "Don't be dramatic. I'm not kicking anyone anywhere but—"

"But what?"

"But a plan will help everyone. Even Luke."

I take in this information, not saying a word, knowing it's not my place.

Honor fills a thermos with coffee, handing it to the man who just upset her. "Take this," she says. "And I'll think about what you've said. I'll make some calls to the YWCA, I heard I might be able to get help with housing."

Jaxon nods. "Thanks, Honor, but you can stay here as long as you need. You are family, and we can make a plan together." Then, clapping me on the back, he says, "Time for us to get to the job site. You ready to start the first day of the rest of your life? Or some shit like that?"

I try not to look at Honor because I know my eyes will betray my feelings for her.

Instead, I will myself to reply nonchalantly. "Sure, some shit like that."

Honor wasn't kidding when she said her life was complicated.

And considering I've fallen for her, mine just got a hell of a lot more complicated, too.

onor

The day goes well...ish. My mind is clouded with the conversation I had with Jaxon about Luke this morning, and the only silver lining I can find is knowing that at the end of the day Hawk is going to walk through that door.

I know it's insanity... thinking about this man this way... but I can't help it. Deep down I know that what we shared wasn't a fleeting moment of passion. He saw my sons this morning and instead of backing away, he greeted me in the kitchen by wrapping his arms around me and calling me Angel.

"Your head's in the clouds, Honor," Harper says, eying me suspiciously. We're folding clothes while the babies are napping and her three-year-olds are playing with Duplos on the carpet in front of us. "What's on your mind?"

I shake my head, not wanting to lie, but most certainly not wanting to discuss Hawk.

49

"Is it about Luke?" she asks. When I don't reply and instead start sorting socks, she sighs. "I can't even imagine what you've been through. And I know Jaxon talked to you this morning about him... I hope it didn't stress you out."

I shrug, not knowing what to say. Of course, it stresses me out. "I don't want the police to get involved."

"We know, but Honor, Luke is irrational. He could show up here and who knows what else? We love you but..."

"But you must protect your family, too." I look over at her triplets, they are so precious to Harper and Jaxon... but my boys are precious to me. And my sister-wives... well, their children are precious to them. Involving the police is going to tear their lives apart. I start crying, not even expecting tears to fall. "It's still just so raw. I'm starting over and am so scared I'm going to mess things up for my boys. I want them to have a better life than I had, but I don't know if I'm strong enough to do that."

"I know sweetie, you're going to need a lot of time to heal, to focus on yourself and your boys. And please, Jaxon is an idiot sometimes—a lot of times—he probably worded things in a way that made you feel like being here has an expiration date. It doesn't." She adds a folded towel to the massive pile. "But maybe talking to Luke isn't the worst idea, maybe he'll lighten up on Jaxon if you do."

"What would you say to him? If you were me?" I ask her, knowing she has a history with him too. Before she married Jaxon, Luke and she were planning on getting married. A real wedding—not a sham marriage like I ended up with.

Harper smirks and tosses her words out easily. "I'd tell him that he should let me go or I'd give him hell. In the form of a police investigation."

I raise a brow. "You know involving the police puts our entire family at risk? Your parents and mine. Not to mention all our siblings." I exhale. "Harper, this isn't something to take lightly."

"I know," she says. "But our parents aren't doing something we condone. They are perpetuating brainwashing. I mean look at my brother. No one even knows where he is. My parents forced him out of the family because he didn't play by their rules. Which is no surprise, they kicked me out a long time ago."

I remember how horrible it was when Harper gave birth to the triplets and her family wrote her off, I remember going to church and being told by her father, the preacher, that I must vow to never speak to his daughter again.

And that was before the church got really nuts and let Luke take over.

But Harper has had more time away from the insanity, and her life has leveled out into something romantic. She squashed her family of origin's horrific theology and created a life for her children that she could be proud of.

I've always looked up to her—which is why I came here in the first place; turned to Harper specifically for help.

The last thing I want to do is cause her and Jaxon problems.

"I'll call Luke," I tell her. "Believe me, I want to push it all behind me as much as anyone."

"I don't blame you. You've been through hell."

"I just want to be happy, you know? Have a partner who respects me, but also cherishes me."

Harper pats my hand. "I know, Honor." She smiles, adding, "Maybe in a few years, after all this is over and you've had a chance to figure out what you want, you can find someone."

"A few years? That seems like a really long time." I twist my lips, knowing I didn't even wait a few weeks.

FRANKIE LOVE

Harper cringes. "Can you imagine getting involved with someone now? What a mess that would be? You need time to get through this without involving a man."

Now it's my turn to smirk. "Says the woman who slept with a stranger the week her wedding got canceled."

Harper blushes. "It's different."

"Oh yeah?" I ask, not giving in to her line of reasoning. "How so?"

"I didn't have kids, for starters. Or a husband."

"Luke was never my husband. He used me; that's it."

"Okay, I get that, but Jaxon and I fell in love really hard, really fast."

"Maybe that could happen to me too," I say softly.

Harper looks at me, sadness written across her face. "I know, sweetie, that would be really wonderful."

"But?"

"But I don't want you to get your hopes up only to watch them fade away."

"Isn't hoping for a fairy tale better than assuming you won't get that happily ever after?"

Harper smiles. "I didn't know you were such a romantic."

"I think every woman is, Harper. But I think a lot of us don't have the luxury of allowing ourselves to daydream. We're so busy surviving, we miss the chance to imagine more for ourselves."

"But now that you've left Luke you can see yourself having more?"

I blink back tears, nodding, thinking of the way Hawk held me last night, cradled in his arms. How he kissed me tenderly, with promise and intention. "Yes, Harper," I tell her. "I see myself having a lot more."

The front door opens then, and Jaxon and Hawk walk in.

I smile broadly, having no intention of waiting a few years for my dream to come true.

Still, I must be cautious. Luke didn't seem like a terrible man until I was living with him... I must make sure Hawk sees me the same way I see him. As something permanent.

awk

The job site is a hell of a lot better than I expected. Wilder and Buck, Jaxon's friends and co-owners of this business, are on a different project today. I work alongside a few other carpenters, Will and Grady, and they are the kind of no bullshit, salt of the earth guys I'm used to working with.

I've spent the last few years under the hood of a car, so I don't know much about swinging a hammer, but still, in some ways being out here in the summer sun, nailing together two by four,is like having a wrench in hand. Both have a singular purpose: to put something in order.

That's why I like to work with my hands. Tools aren't complicated like people, and I can mind my own business, yet still end a workday feeling like I've accomplished something.

But as I walk back into Jaxon and Harper's house I know my life is more complicated than it's ever been.

All day, thoughts of Honor and her sons crowd my mind. I sure as hell didn't want to raise any suspicion by asking Jaxon any details, but his words about her husband are fucking ringing in my ear.

Still, I tried my damnedest to focus on the job today. We're renovating a cabin on a piece of land Jaxon got for a steal. He plans on selling this home as soon as it's finished for a sweet profit.

And for most of the day, I could push aside my memory of last night, Honor lying under me in the bed of my truck, under the starlit sky. It was fucking hard, but I managed, knowing I wanted to do a good job for my cousin who fucking bailed me out of jail a week ago.

But now we're home, walking into the living room where Harper and Honor are standing, and all I want to do is wrap my arms around Honor, ask her about her day, slip off her shoes and rub her feet and treat her like the princess she is.

I don't know why I'm so insanely attracted to this woman —I know she has more baggage than I've ever dreamed of carrying, and as I look at her now, her curvy hips and swollen breasts, her round ass and long hair— I know I'm turned on by her physically.

But physical attraction has never been enough for me— no woman has made me want to pack it in and claim her as my own... but Honor is more than beautiful.

She is the woman who was made for me.

And when Honor smiles at the son in her arms, beaming at his big belly laugh, and she tickles him, making his laughter even louder, it's impossible not to be drawn toward her energy, her force field—her essence. Honor looks over at me, our eyes lock.

She knows this as deeply as I do.

This is not about one night of passion.

This is about more than sex. About lust. About wanting my cock buried in her perfect pussy.

This is about something real.

But I can't draw attention to how I feel. Not right now. Not with Harper and Jaxon watching. No way in hell they would understand.

"Hey, baby," Jaxon says, walking over to Harper. As he wraps her in his arms, his triplets come running over, shouting for Daddy. He pulls them in for a bear hug, then lets them wrestle him to the ground.

Honor's eyes meet mine, and I refuse to look away. I want to see her, feel her emotions, understand everything there is to know about her.

"What?" she says, softly, as if embarrassed by my intent gaze.

I raise my brows and shake my head in a smirk. "Your babies asleep?"

She nods yes, stepping around the piles of folded laundry and coming closer to me, giving Jaxon and his family more privacy. They seem caught up in one another, though and don't even notice us as we walk toward the kitchen.

I grab a glass of water and Honor watches me as I do, and I have the sensation that she is memorizing my movements. I understand. I'm doing the exact same thing to her.

Before we can start a conversation, though, babies start crying from all over the house. Harper has a two-year-old and a one-year-old, and Honor has three... that's a lot of crying babies in case anyone was wondering.

"That's my cue," she says, tapping her fingers on the granite counter top.

"Do you need help?" I ask.

She looks at me doubtfully. Eventually, she shakes her head. "It's not that I don't want your help—but you need to get yourself cleaned up." I look down at myself and know she's right. After working outside all day my clothes are sweaty and covered in sawdust and dirt. "Besides," she adds, "my boys are pretty particular about which hands hold them right now. It's been a long week."

"Sounds like it's been a long year."

She nods. "A long everything."

I nod, not taking the fact that she needs to get her babies on her own personally. But damn, one day in and I'm utterly under Honor's spell. I want to be more for her. Everything for her.

But I also want to respect her space. She's the mother, she knows what her children need. And right now, they need her.

—

The evening disappears in a flash. With Jaxon's five and Honor's three, that's eight kids living here right now. The fact anyone has time to have sex is a fucking miracle.

Jaxon hands me a beer after the last of his kids are in bed. He looks exhausted, but there is still a smile on his face. I know how hard he worked on the job site all day, and that's nothing compared to how hard Harper must have worked back here at the house. The fact that they still laugh and kiss is a goddamned miracle as far as I'm concerned. These kids are a hell of a lot of work.

Harper walks into the kitchen, her hair's in a messy bun, she's wearing sweats and a hoodie—the look of a woman who deserves however much wine she wants tonight. But she doesn't look spent... she looks like she's ready for an evening with her husband. Earlier I heard them discussing the night's plan to keep marathoning through The Walking Dead.

Romance at its motherfucking best.

FRANKIE LOVE

"After a night with us, I bet you're ready to go get sterilized," Jaxon says, laughing. Harper laughs too, as she pours herself a glass of white wine.

I shrug at Jaxon's comment, feeling the heat rise to my cheeks. Thank God I have a beard big enough to hide some of my emotion. The truth is I want Honor to have my children. I want to fill her with my seed and watch her belly blossom. I want to take care of her; of all of her children, make us a family.

And that's after just one day with her.

"I don't know, man," I tell him. "Sure, you and Harper look exhausted—but it's a good exhaustion."

Jaxon and Harper smile at this, she raises her glass to her husband's bottle. "Cheers to the sweet labor of love," she says.

I take a swig of my beer and can't help but think this is what I've been missing all my life. I've been fucking around, getting in trouble, trying to help my friends—people who could have found a way to help themselves.

I know I have a soft spot for taking care of people. But maybe that's why my heart is so open to Honor right now. I'm good at fighting injustice, for taking my friends who are down-on-their-luck under my wing. I'll stick up for the weary. Hell, I'll go to jail for them. Now, though, for the first time in my life, I want to put all that good intention in the right place.

There is only one place I feel like it belongs. With the woman who captured my heart with one glance. Who I fell for before I even knew her name.

Just then, Honor walks in the room, a crying infant in her arms. She doesn't look the good kind of exhausted. She just looks worn out.

"Hey, sweetie," Harper says, frowning. "Titus giving you a run for your money?"

"Yeah," she says. "Every time I try to lay him down

58

without me, he starts up again. I think I'm just gonna call it a night, okay? I'll go to bed with him, that way the rest of the tribe can stay asleep."

"You sure?" Harper asks. "We don't mind him staying up with us. We're gonna turn on Netflix."

"No." Honor tries to smile, but it's grim. "I don't think the zombie apocalypse is going to help Titus fall asleep."

"We could put on something else?" Jaxon asks.

Honor shakes her head. "No way—this is your time. And honestly, I'm exhausted."

"Okay," Harper says, biting her lip. "Sleep well."

"Goodnight." Honor waves with her free hand, and as she leaves I feel her heart breaking just a bit with each step she takes.

I watch her leave, and I swear she gives me the slightest nod, toward her door, before turning to Harper and Jaxon myself.

"I'm gonna call it a night myself," I tell them.

"You sure? It's only 8:30," Jaxon says.

"I'm sure. I'm not used to all this back-breaking work."

"Alright man. See ya in the morning."

I head to my room, biding my time for when Honor's kids fall asleep, knowing that once they are down for the count, I'm going to help put a smile back on my angel's face.

CHAPTER 12

onor

Titus is finally drunk on mama milk and sound asleep. Only took two hours. I blink, knowing what I need right now is a shower before I go to bed myself. It's been a long 24 hours.

I ease him from my mattress and set him in the Pack 'n Play. His little hands are tucked under his chin, and I could melt from looking at his perfection. I'm so grateful for my children, but my heart? It's so tender right now.

Knowing my children won't have a father to watch them grow up is so sad—especially since my choices and my lack of bravery for so long is what made this happen. I should have been wiser years ago.

Should have run before I was ensnared by a man like Luke.

I grab my bathrobe from a hook and open the bathroom door. Swallowing my shame, I remind myself that I did the best I could. I am doing the best I can.

I know I need to call Luke. Harper and Jaxon both want me to. But I'm not ready. Not yet. It's only been a week. And I know how persuasive he is. He can lay on the guilt like nobody's business—how else would he have convinced so many people to change their religious views? He is a wheeler and a dealer.

And a cheat.

The images of him cheating on me... and on True and Kind... with another woman... are permanently glued in my mind. He says he was going to marry the prostitute, make her his fourth wife, but I wasn't going to stay around and watch that happen.

Those memories fade away, however, as I step into the bathroom and see Hawk standing here.

In nothing but boxers.

The lighting is low. The bath is full of bubbles. Candles are lit. His eyes are on mine.

"Did I interrupt something?" I ask, poorly hiding a smile.

My heart thrums with pleasure, the sadness that had been filling me as I put Titus to sleep slips away.

How could any woman be sad with this romantic gesture before them?

"Angel, you didn't interrupt anything at all. I was getting this ready for you." Hawk steps toward me and brushes a loose tendril of hair from my face. "You look exhausted, completely worn out. I hate to see you like this."

He cups my face and I lean into his palm. Feeling him cradle my cheek is so comforting, so utterly soothing.

"It's been hard moving here," I admit. "I wanted to talk to you earlier, about the cult ... about everything, but it was impossible with Jaxon and Harper here. I didn't want you to find out about my past like you did this morning. When Jaxon was talking to me... I was scared you'd heard too much... and that you would be done with me."

Hawk shakes his head softly, "Hush," he says. "You don't need to justify anything to me. Who you are is enough. I'm just grateful to be with you right now."

"A week ago, I was sharing a house with a man and two of his other wives. When I said my life is complicated, I wasn't exaggerating."

"Hey, I get that, I have so much to learn about you, about your past, about your future. What you want for your life. But we don't need to talk about all that right now. Your eyes are filled with exhaustion, and I'm guessing your body needs to relax. I was thinking you could take this bath and have some alone time. You deserve it, Honor."

I feel heat rise to my cheeks and I bite my bottom lip.

"What is it?" he asks, resting his forehead on mine. The movement is so intimate, it makes my core tighten, my panties soaked. A man has never been like this with me before. So completely patient.

"I want to relax," I tell him. "And I am exhausted. But I don't want to take this bath by myself. I want you, too..."

I don't finish the sentence because it feels so brazen to say what my body wants. Who am I to talk like that, to ask for what I desire?

"You don't need to be embarrassed with me," he says. "Hell, I've done enough things to embarrass both of us. There's nothing you can say or do that's gonna make me think less of you. Because right now I feel like I see you for what you are."

"Yeah?" I lick my lips, not sure how he sees me. "And what's that, Hawk?" My words are merely a whisper on my lips.

I want to know how Hawk sees me, and at the same time, I don't want him to say a word. Part of me is scared that if he tells me how he feels about me, I'll be let down.

Because I've known him for one single day, but my feelings are deep and wide.

"I see you as a gentle woman, wise beyond your years. I watched you tonight, cradling your babies in your arms, soothing them with your words. Patience pouring out of you. But you let all that goodness drain you until there was nothing left."

"You don't understand, Hawk. It's not that I don't want to keep some of that for myself, but I'm alone in this world. And no one is here to help pick up the pieces of my broken life. I have to give everything I've got to my sons because no one else is here to help me."

Hawk's jaw tenses, he looks at me with intention, desire. Truth.

"Let me help you. For as long as we have. Let me help you."

I shake my head, wanting him so badly, but not wanting to take more than I ought. Scared to death that he is going to hurt me like Luke did.

I protect myself with my words, "I don't know anything about you."

He scoffs immediately as if my words are ridiculous. "Does that matter right now?" he asks.

He says it so plainly, I'm forced to respond. Forced to answer in truth.

And the truth is, it doesn't matter. I don't care about Hawk's past—and not in a dismissive way. In an accepting way.

I want his help.

And what is that? Accepting someone's grace, when you don't even know them? And more than that—what does it say about Hawk, being so willing to offer it?

I swallow because deep down I know exactly what that is.

It is love.

63

I blink, feeling like that word is ridiculous in this moment. A man like Hawk can't love a woman like me. But oh, how my heart is pulled toward him.

My own feelings seem so reckless. How can I consider love when my life is in such a state of disrepair?

Harper seemed to hit the nail on the head earlier today. I'm in no place to start something with a man.

But then I look up at Hawk's cloudy gray eyes; he's waiting for an answer. "I'll ask you again, Angel," he says. "You don't know much about me, but does that matter right now?"

I shake my head and I wrap my arms around his neck. "Right now, all that matters is this."

And I press my mouth against his, his soft lips somehow firm against mine. This kiss steadies me, holds me in place.

And yet, manages to take my breath away; manages to let my fears float into the oblivion.

In place of the fear, all that is left in this candlelit bathroom is a flicker of love.

CHAPTER 13

awk

It doesn't take long to get her out of her clothes, and when she pulls her tank top off over her head, I see her beautiful breasts for the first time.

Damn, looking at her topless, I know she is more than a woman. She is a mother. And her breasts, the ones that give life to her babies, are full and gorgeous, generous globes of pure pleasure.

She covers herself with her palms, her fingers brushing against her hard nipples, then letting her fingers roam lower, grazing down toward her beautiful pussy.

"You don't need to be embarrassed around me, remember?" I tell her. "I thought we just covered that."

In the soft candlelit glow of the bathroom, I see her cheeks flush pale pink and she bites her bottom lip, having no idea how fucking hot she looks right now.

A real woman before me, her body has been given as an

offering of love to her sons. Still, no matter how much of a woman she is, I know her heart is still so fragile and I don't fucking take that lightly. I take it like the gift it is.

Honor has been through way too much and the last thing I'm going to do is hurt her. Honor deserves a life full of bubble baths and candlelight and romance.

"If you're telling me to not be embarrassed, I'm wondering why your boxers are still on?" She raises an eyebrow toward me and moves her hands to her hips, and when she does her body is revealed in all its glory.

"You know the moment I take these boxers off my cock is going to jump out and scare you." I laugh softly and she just shakes her head.

Her lips turn to a smile. "I don't scare easily."

I take a step toward her, I'm not going to hold back if she gives me the go-ahead.

I drop my boxers and start stroking my long, hard shaft.

"Last night was so fucking hot," I tell her. I remember fucking her in the back of my truck, filling her up with my length, and damn I'm hard as a rock thinking about it again.

"I've obviously had sex, more than I would have liked, but Hawk, what you did to me last night..." She stops, and I see tears in her eyes. I brush one away with my thumb. "When you touched me last night," she says, "it made me feel so beautiful."

"Good. That's how you deserve to feel. Forever."

Honor laughs quietly. "You've known me a day and already telling me how I should feel forever?" She closes her eyes and exhales. "This all feels like a dream, Hawk. Like, it's too good to be true."

I know I need to tell her why I ended up here. I need to explain my past and let her know that I may see her as the most beautiful thing in the world, but I've got a dark past; have a track record that isn't anything I'm proud of. I don't

want to tell her that tonight because it will fill her heart with
worry, it will cause her brows to crease, a frown to form, and
right now this woman doesn't need to feel anything but
blissed out.

I pull her toward me, my cock hard against her belly, and
I kiss her harder, more deeply, my hands are in her hair, and
her arms are around my neck. I just want to be closer, closer.
Close enough to devour her.

She's whimpering against my mouth, so desperate for
pleasure.

"Do you think Harper will hear?" she asks, pulling away
mid-kiss.

I shake my head. "Jaxon and Harper are busy watching a
show about fucking zombies. They're in their own world.
And we are in ours."

She looks at the bathroom door, leading to her bedroom.
It's open a crack, and there isn't a single noise from inside.

"You sure you're okay with this?" I ask.

Her eyes brighten, reassuring me that she wants this as
badly as I do.

"Make love to me in the bathtub," she says, running her
finger down my chest. "I've never done that before."

I grin, loving the fact that Harper and Jaxon put in a
Jacuzzi tub here. It's big enough for the two of us.

As we step into the hot water, Honor's shoulders relax
instantly, and she sinks down into the bubbles.

"Oh, this feels so good," she says.

I pull her toward me and she lies against my chest.
Having her close like this is more than I ever imagined for
myself. With this woman, here in my arms, I want to be a
better man.

"I've never taken a bath with a woman, so this is a first for
both of us."

She laughs. "That surprises me, that we found a first to

share. It seems like... with my story and... whatever your story is... I was kind of thinking that between the two of us we've seen it all."

"I have a feeling there's a lot of firsts we could share."

I swallow, feeling her soft skin against mine.

Sure, I slept with a bunch of women, but I never made love to anyone but her. And yes, I've been through the wringer with the law, but I've never had a reason to be a real man. To step up and create a life that mattered.

"Is it crazy?" she asks. "That I want to have a lot of firsts with you?"

"It's not crazy at all," I tell her. I press my fingers to her pussy and as I touch her, her soft folds open to me. And when she slides over my cock, rocking against me, it's like she is ready to be filled up completely. I run my hands over her ass and pull her closer still. She sinks down on my cock, eyes closed as she does. Her breasts are round, her ass is perfect, her body made to bring forth life. To give pleasure. I don't want her to experience any more pain.

I make love to Honor, my cock deep inside of her and she pants above me, her breasts bouncing slowly as she moves over me, grinding against me until she's tipping over into an orgasm.

"Oh Hawk, oh, I'm so close," she moans.

I fill her up, thrusting deep inside of her, exploding in her pussy the way she wants, the way I need.

"Oh, baby," I manage, catching my breath, my cock still pounding inside of her, our bodies hot and full of passion. "Angel, this is everything."

She nods wordlessly because she knows that's the absolute truth. She smiles then as if she has something to say that's going to make me happy.

"It was good, right?" I ask.

She nods, pulling from me and sitting opposite me in the

tub. Our bodies are red from the hot water, and she twists her hair up on her head, wrapping an elastic band around it. "I'm so hot. Literally. Could use a cool shower." She smiles. "So... I was thinking."

"Oh yeah?"

"Well, I've never taken a shower with a man either. I think we should have another first."

I grin, loving the way this woman thinks. I stand and take her hand. I may have showered with a woman before, but never with Honor. Never with the woman, I'm going to make my wife.

 onor

For the next week, I'm in a blissed-out state of euphoria.

Suddenly taking care of these children isn't anywhere near as demanding... because after they go to sleep each night I sneak away into the bathroom or into Hawk's bedroom and we talk for hours. We make love for hours.

In doing so, we learn the hard facts about our pasts, but somehow, they're made lighter because they have been shared with someone else.

When Hawk tells me about his track record, about being in jail half a dozen times, for getting arrested for breaking and entering, for the bar fights and the stolen cars... about his mom killing an innocent person, and how it messed with his head. There are a lot of tears on my part.

But there is a lot of forgiveness too.

I can see that beneath the list of crimes, they were all committed as acts of love.

The stolen car was really just a case of being at the wrong place at the wrong time. His buddy had bought the car—not knowing it was stolen. When they found out, Hawk attempted to return it to its rightful owner—which is when he was pulled over by the cops.

And the breaking and entering? His buddy had split up with his girlfriend, and the ex refused to give him back his toolbox. Something essential for a man like Hawk and his friends, who work on cars day and night. Hawk went with his buddy to the girl's place, to get back the toolbox from her garage.

And the cops were called.

The bar fight, that makes make sense, too. Hawk was sticking up for people who were getting messed with. And Hawk, being tall and strong and capable didn't seem to want to watch his friends being beat to a pulp. So, he stepped in. He took hits, he rolled with the punches.

I'm not an idiot, I can see how someone could hear these facts, and think I am justifying, or making excuses for Hawk. But I was lying beside him in his bed as he recounted the stories with honesty and integrity. I can't help but feel that he is a misunderstood man.

And maybe it's crazy, to think I am the woman who can understand him... But I do. I am.

In the same way, he lets my tears fall against his chest as I tell him the painful facts of my fake marriage. The condemnation, and the judgment I felt every day.

He asks, "But do you believe in a God that would let this happen? Do you believe in God at all?" His room is dark, the lights are off, and there is nothing to see but the truth.

"I believe in love," I tell him. "I believe in hope. I believe in the promise of a better life."

"It sounds like you're avoiding the question." Hawk doesn't beat around the bush, he wants to understand things completely before he gives his opinion. I love that about him: he doesn't jump to conclusions about people—the exact opposite of my ex.

"Hawk, I believe in God, but not the kind of God Luke forced me to pray to. I believe in something eternal; I believe in destiny. I believe that because I found you, we were brought together. This has to be divine intervention."

Hawk kisses my forehead, his arms wrap around me, pulling me closer. "I don't know if it was God, but I think it was certainly fate."

It's always like this with Hawk. For the last eight days, we've spent hours upon hours hashing out what we want, what we believe, who we are... Who we wish to be.

But I know disappearing into his arms and body every night isn't everything. The nighttime hours feel like I'm dreaming, and when I wake each morning and have Harper and Jaxon gently pressuring me to call Luke, I know I can't stave them off forever. They deserve more than that. They deserve to have my situation with Luke taking care of.

Today, I'm going to call him. I don't tell Hawk this because part of me is so ashamed of the marriage I had with Luke that I don't want anyone else to hear our conversation. Even if I trust Hawk–and I do–it doesn't take away the reality that this is a mess I made. Hawk shouldn't have to clean it up.

The babies are napping and Harper and I are cleaning up lunch. Rosie and Stella's families are coming over tonight for dinner, we're having a big barbecue outside. We have a big list of things to do before the babies wake up and the others arrive. There are baked beans in the crockpot, but we need to finish the sides and make the hamburger patties.

"So, I'm gonna start with the coleslaw, do you want to do the potato salad?" Harper asks.

"Yeah, of course. But first I'm gonna make a phone call. The one I've been putting off for a while."

Harper raises an eyebrow. "Are you gonna call Luke?"

I nod. "I know I've been putting it off all week, and it's not fair to you or anybody really. So, I need to call him, and at least try to convince them to stop harassing you guys."

"Do you want to talk on speakerphone, so someone else hears..."

I shake my head. "I need to do this myself. I need to figure out a way to be strong with him. Because all I've ever been is weak."

Harper nods and I know she understands this. It took strength for her to walk away from her family, stay away from Luke. She knows that this isn't easy.

"Okay sweetie," she says, squeezing my shoulder. "I'm here for you. Whatever you need. We're all here for you."

I nod, appreciating how understanding she is. I step out to the back porch. The deck is beautiful, huge and plenty of space for all the tables that will be set out tonight.

I take a seat in an Adirondack chair and pull the flip phone from my pocket. Pressing Luke's number into it, I hold the phone to my ear, steeling myself for whatever comes next.

"Hello? Who is this?" Luke asks into the phone.

I take a deep breath. "It's me. Honor."

"It about time, you little heathen."

"Don't, please. Don't start like that,"

"How would you like me to start, Honor? You ran away from everything you know is true and right. The church. And you left with my children."

"You don't care about the boys, you only care about yourself."

"Don't get short with me. How dare you run off to a place like Jaxon and Harper's? You know how evil they are."

73

FRANKIE LOVE

I look around Jaxon and Harper's beautiful property. Acres and acres of forests, wildflowers growing in their lawn, a gorgeous swing set situated to the left, and a fire pit on the right. It's an idyllic place, a place full of love and companionship. A place a family belongs.

"I don't want to talk about Jaxon and Harper. I want to talk about us."

"Oh, that's rich, Honor. I don't want to talk to you at all. I want you to get yourself in the van and bring home my children. I need you here where you belong."

My fingers wrap tight around the phone, my knuckles white. My blood thick. "I'm not coming home, Luke. I'm not coming back to you. We're done."

"Like hell we are. You're my wife, and I can't have my congregation see that you left me."

"Where do they think I am right now?"

"You are visiting a suffering cousin."

"Oh, and Harper is the suffering cousin? It's ridiculous. I came here because she was the only—person—who would accept me."

"You need to get home."

"Or what? What are you gonna do? You want me to go to the police?"

"I know you won't go to the police. Because you have a bleeding heart; because you know what that will mean for your family, for True and for Kind—and their children. You're not going to let them be split apart, their homes to be ruined."

"You don't know anything about me or what I'm capable of," I tell him.

"I'm coming for you in a week. You don't want to come back? Fine, I'll drive to that place myself and I'll put those children into the van and I will drive you home. Do you understand?"

74

Tears stream down my face, he knows me all too well. I don't want him to know me at all. "You won't, you won't really come here."

"Yes, I will. And I know you won't really go to the cops."

"Jaxon needs you to stop calling him. You need you to stop it, Luke, please." I know I'm trying to reason with a madman, but I have no other choice. I don't want to go to the cops. It's the last thing I want. It would ruin so much for the people I still love. People who don't seem strong enough to leave yet.

I'd rather slowly help Kind and True find a new life for themselves, not rip their children from their arms and be sent to child protective services. That's what would happen if I called the cops right now, and they broke up this church that Luke has created.

Luke knows that.

"Luke, just give me two weeks. Two weeks where you promise you won't call Jaxon. I can't have you coming yet. I need more time... Please?"

I can practically hear Luke's fury over the phone call. "Two weeks. Two weeks and that's it. You've had your time off playing, tramping around like a little whore. But you know where you belong. Here with your children and sister-wives. Who are you to take our boys from their father? You don't have it in you. Two weeks. That's it. And then I'm coming and I'm getting you. And you're coming home where you belong."

I'm shaking, but two weeks is better than nothing. In two weeks' time, maybe I can figure out a future for myself. A future that doesn't involve the police.

I blink, squeezing my eye shut, thinking of Hawk... wanting a future with him, but knowing Hawk doesn't even have a house. He can't take me and my children under his wing. There is an expiration date to this dream. To this

75

fantasy. Do I want to say in this fantasy forever? Of course, I do. But the reality is I have three mouths to feed. And I can't stay at Harper and Jaxon's forever.

"Fine," I tell him. "Two weeks. Two weeks and then—"

"And then I'm going to bring you home."

I drop the phone on the deck, it skitters across the patio before coming to a stop. My heart stops too.

I have two weeks before I have to say goodbye to a life that was never mine in the first place.

CHAPTER 15

awk

The moment I get home from work, I see that Honor's a mess.

My heart goes out to her. Tonight is all about having a little fun, friends coming over and having a barbecue.

But Honor is all bent out of shape.

It's unusual for her. I've watched her the last week, and it seems no matter what, Honor can take whatever life throws at her in stride, but not right now. Right now, she's in pain.

Rosie and Buck and their kids are streaming into the house, along with Stella and Wilder's family, and I do my best to motion to her discreetly to join me in our shared bathroom so I can hear how her day has been, but we keep getting cut off.

Rosie wraps Honor in a hug, asking about her potato salad recipe, and Wilder and Buck drag me out to the back deck, handing me a beer.

"This job is a killer in July, isn't it?" Buck asks.

"Sure is," I tell him. "But it's good to be outside. Never thought I'd say it, but I don't even miss being under the hood of a car."

"I hear ya," Buck says. "I ran a grocery store for a few years, down in town, but was never satisfied. Then I decided to start doing my wood carving, and I made a good living off it, thought I'd finally found my thing—but then Jaxon handed me a hammer. I built a home and I never looked back. There's something about creating a place for a family to live that is more meaningful than any other work I've done."

Dean laughs. "Damn, we should get that TV crew back out here, record you waxing poetic."

"Fuck off," Buck says, a grin on his face. "We don't need a TV crew back here, ever."

"Agreed. Hell, we've all found our women, we don't need anything else."

The guys look at me, shrugging. "Well, I guess you still need to find yourself a nice girl," Buck says.

Jaxon frowns. "Eh, Hawk is still young. What are you, barely 24?"

I nod.

"Yeah, you need to spend more time sowing your wild oats."

I want to tell them I don't have anything to sow— that I already found my woman— but I know Honor would hate that. She isn't ready to be open about our relationship— and honestly, I'm not either. I love our little cocoon every night and don't exactly want to fuck up that precious ecosystem we've just begun to build.

Dean claps me on the back. "In five years then, you can settle down."

I cock a brow at him. "You think you know what I need?"

Jaxon laughs. "I know what you need. I bet two weeks

without a woman in your bed is longer than you've ever gone."

The guys all laugh at this, and I just shake my head.

"Regardless," I say. "I really do love the work. And I'd never have considered it if I hadn't gotten myself in such a mess."

"Is it all sorted now?" Buck asks.

I nod. "Yeah, I met with the judge before I came out here and the other guy dropped the charges, thank God. I didn't want to lose my savings over an asshole in a bar."

"You bang the guy up pretty good?" Buck asks.

I shrug. "He got some stitches; he's fine. And hell, he started it."

"Good to hear, man," Wilder says. "We're always looking for full-time men to join the crew."

Jax laughs. "He's been here a week. Let's see how he's feeling in a month, okay?"

I raise my empty bottle and head to the cooler to grab another. As I do, I see Rosie and Stella deep in conversation with Honor over by the swing set. The women each have a baby in their arms, but you can tell they are talking heatedly.

Harper is walking toward the guys with a fussing baby in her arms, I stop her and ask what the girls are talking about.

"You want the gossip?" Harper laughs, handing me Honor's son Timothy. "Then hold him and let me get a glass of wine."

I pat Tim's back, bouncing him gently. He laughs at me, clapping his hands together.

"Look at you," Harper says, returning with a glass of white wine. "You're a natural."

I swallow hard, choking on her words. They are words that I fucking love to hear. I want to be a natural at this. The kind of man Honor needs to help raise her children.

"So, what's the story?" I ask, nodding toward the women.

"Well, Honor called her ex today. She told him she'd go back in two weeks."

I pull back, the words shocking me. "No way," I say. "I don't believe it."

Honor shakes her head. "Right? It's the truth, though, she talked to Luke and he told her she needed to come back, then she came to me and told me everything. I really thought I'd convinced her to stay, to let the police get involved, but then her sister-wives called."

"Hell," I say, knowing this isn't going to end well.

"Yeah, well, they told her that Luke has been horrible to them since she left, how they need her back so Luke will calm down."

I run my hand over my beard, imagining Honor going through this today. It eats me up inside.

"So now what?" I ask.

"Now she feels awful. She says staying here is selfish."

"But what about her boys?" I ask, my voice louder than I intended. "She can't go back and do that to them."

Harper raises an eyebrow. "I know, Benjamin. But it's not our life. The kids aren't being beaten, she swears Luke has never laid a hand on her."

"Emotional abuse is abuse, too."

Harper's eyes narrow. "I know. I used to be engaged to the man. I know what being with him is like. But if she goes to the police so many families will be ripped apart."

"You're being weak. You should go to the cops now."

"And say what?" Harper scoffs. "Tell them a man is cheating on his wife? True is the only one he's legally married to."

"Did your father take other wives? Or any other church members?"

Harper sighs. "I think so. But honestly, I haven't talked to my parents in years. I was excommunicated."

"See, then how you can just stand by—"

"I'm not standing by anything. It's just a lot more complicated than telling the cops. You wouldn't understand. You are too young and haven't been through—"

"We're the same age, Harper. And just because my family never joined a cult, it doesn't mean I don't understand life being complicated. I just don't want Honor to go back there."

Harper sighs, blinking back tears. "I know. I just want Honor to stay here and away from men altogether."

"You mean away from Luke?"

Harper shrugs sadly. "Away from anyone and anything that's going to distract her from getting her life back together. She'll need a way to provide for herself eventually. She needs to call social services. They'll help her with housing and job training."

I hate that idea. Honor moving away, to the city where public housing is. I want her here on this mountain.

I want her here with me.

I sure as hell don't want her back with Luke.

 onor

For the next week, I avoid the reality of the ticking time clock of my life.

Hawk tries to comfort me, reason with me... but it's hard to talk about my situation without getting emotional.

"I just can't imagine how you would choose that, knowing what you do." Hawk shakes his head at me as he paces around his bedroom. It's late at night and Timothy is in his arms. Hawk pats his back, soothing him. He woke up crying and found comfort in the arms of the very same man I find comforting.

I watch Hawk pace the bedroom without a shirt on, the lamplight casting a warm glow across the room, and see my little baby boy suck on his thumb and nestle deeper against Hawk's chest.

"It's not as simple as what I want. It's not just me. How many times do I have to say that?" I'm explaining the same thing over and over to him. "You could never understand because you've never met my sister-wives. They may be judgmental women, but it is because they are so confused. They are so much like me, in their twenties, their arms full of babies, brainwashed into believing things about themselves that just aren't true."

"Don't you want more for them?" Hawk asks.

I close my eyes. "I hate that you think I'm being weak right now because the truth is, Hawk, this is me being strong."

"Sacrificing yourself isn't always strength."

"It is," I tell him, my voice in a loud whisper.

"Maybe for some people, but not for you, Honor. That's not what this is about."

"What is it about then?" I ask.

"It's about you being scared to take what you really want, what you are so close to having. Are you gonna throw it all away for Luke? It's bullshit, Honor."

"You're gonna wake up Timothy," I say, taking my baby from his arms, and carry him through the bathroom back to his crib. I set him down in his Pack 'n Play and he curls up into a ball and goes back to sleep. I sigh deeply, so frustrated that Hawk and I aren't seeing eye to eye.

But unless Hawk wants to take care of me and the boys... I can't see a future with him. Not now, not like this. We can't stay at Jaxon and Harper's place forever.

"Honor," he says, walking back into my bedroom. "Baby, it's gonna be okay." He pulls me into a hug, and we stand in my bedroom, the queen-size bed flanked by cribs on either side. This room is so full.

Full of pain for the past. And full of fear for our future. I close my eyes, breathing him in. Not wanting to let go.

He wraps his arms more tightly around me, tucks a strand of hair behind my ear. "I love you, Honor," he tells me.

The room is so quiet; all I hear is the breathing of my boys. The beating heart of my man. And I don't want to go back to Luke. Imagining True and Kind's life is painful, picturing them being at the mercy of a man who is full of anger... but then I imagine my life.

And I know who I want.

What I want.

For me, and for my boys.

"Did you hear me?" he says again.

"I love you, too." I muffle a sob into his chest, he smells like strength and steadies me like an anchor.

"I loved you the moment I saw you," he tells me, kissing my forehead, refusing to let me go.

"You're not just saying that, so I won't go back to Luke?"

He rests his chin atop my head. "I'm not just saying that for anything. It's the goddamn truth, Honor. I love you. And I don't know how to take care of you yet, but that's what I want to do. And I want to figure out how to be the man you need."

Tears stream down my face. I'm scared my crying is going to wake up the babies, so I take his hand and guide him back to his bedroom.

In his room, I turn off the lamp and I let my bathrobe fall to the ground, let him pull me to him. And in seconds both of us are in the bed, tangled around one another, our confession propelling us toward the physical manifestation of our love.

His mouth is on my breasts, on my belly, on my entrance, between my thighs. His tongue licks me, my wetness seeping against his beard, and him lapping it all up. His tongue flicks over my clit and I wrap my legs around his head, bringing my core closer to him as he devours me. His tongue flicks against me, causing a cascade of pleasure to roll through my body. My back arches, my body held by his hands. He pushes down my knees, licking me more completely, sucking on me until there is nothing left for my body to do but cry out in ecstasy.

His hand covers my mouth as he tries to hide my screams, but the orgasm is rushing over me so hard, so fast. His eyes are on mine and he says again, "I love you, Honor."

I squeeze my eyes shut tight, feeling the tears streaming down my face.

I nod and he moves his hand away.

"I love you, too," I tell him between the tears and pleasure and the relief and the truth. I love him in ways that feel too good to be true. More than I deserve or ever expected. I love him and he loves me and I come hard, against him. I come hard, with him.

I reach for his cock, stroking the long shaft, feeling how velvety smooth he is, my body wanting his so badly. Now and forever and for always.

His balls are tight in my hand and everything about his cock makes my body excited. When he fills me up I feel so good. I need to feel that way right now. He pulls me over onto all fours, runs his hand over my ass, between my legs, feeling my wetness. He cups my pussy like it is his, his fingers pressing inside of me, and I moan as he touches me so perfectly. I feel his cock edging against my ass.

"Is your pussy ready for me?" he asks.

I grin, feeling so good. "My pussy was made ready for you. It loves you. Just like I do," I tell him as he presses himself inside of me, my arms resting on the pillow, and I try to muffle my voice as I moan, loudly.

"Yes, Hawk," I whimper. "Yes, baby, fill me like the bad boy you are." My body shakes as he thrusts deep inside of me.

His hands are on my waist as he plows into my pussy, just like he likes it, just the way I need it.

"I love you so fucking much," he tells me.

I pull up on my knees, my hands over my head reaching

for his face, pulling him toward my neck and he kisses my ears and my shoulders, his hands cradling my breasts, pulling himself hard against me.

Together we come, him filling me with his creamy release over and over again. Our bodies are slick with sweat, drenched in pleasure. The memory of pain floating away from us like a distant memory. It's as if the only thing we've ever experienced is absolute perfection.

"I fucking love you," Hawk says as he comes in me with a crash. My pussy drips with pleasure, my body on fire.

"I love you too, baby. Yes, yes, yes," I cry, this time my pleasure isn't muffled by anything. This time my pleasure is revealed. And with Hawk deep inside me, both of us naked, in love, and dripping wet, his bedroom door flings opens.

"What the fuck?" Jaxon hollers, walking in on us.

I fall to the bed, Hawk's thickness pulling from me.

He told me he loves me and now there's going to be hell to pay.

CHAPTER 17

$\mathcal{H}$awk

I knew our nightly rendezvous was eventually gonna bite us in the ass. I didn't think it was going to happen when I was literally holding onto her ass, fucking her from behind.

But now she's wrapped up in a sheet on my bed, and I'm pulling on my boxers as Harper and Jaxon enter the bedroom side by side.

"Benjamin, are you kidding me with this?" Harper asks. She grabs Jaxon's arm, trying to make sense of what she sees.

"Give us a second," I say, not wanting them to see the woman I love in such disarray.

"You want a second?" Jaxon asks. "I let you stay in my home, I trusted you. You're working on my crew by day and at night you're fucking Honor? You know how much she's been through, the last thing she needs is—"

Honor raises her voice and cuts him off. "You don't know what I need, Jaxon. I need Hawk." Honor clutches the bed sheets around her as Harper flicks on the light, and its glare falls across all four of us.

The same way I'm glaring at Jaxon now.

"This is ridiculous, Honor, go to bed. And you, Hawk, I want to see you outside," Jaxon yells.

I don't give a fuck what he wants right now. "You can't talk to her that way," I growl at him. "*That's* the last fucking thing Honor needs."

Jaxon laughs sharply. "Oh, as if you know what she needs?" He says it so dismissively as if I couldn't have a motherfucking clue.

That's the problem with Jaxon, though; he thinks he knows what he just walked in on, but he has no clue. I promised to take care of Honor and her babies, and I'm not taking that lightly.

"I don't want to fight," Honor says. "The kids are asleep. I just wanted..." Honor wraps the sheet around her and runs from the room toward her bathroom locking the door. I look at Harper and Jaxon, shaking my head. "Is that what you wanted to have happen? Honor felt safe with me—"

Harper cuts me off. "It's because you've tricked her. She's vulnerable right now, Ben. You don't actually want to take care of her. You just want to have a good time." Her eyes are fierce. I understand why she's being protective of Honor, but her desire to protect is getting in the way of reason.

"I can't have you here. I can't have you in this house if you're using her this way," Jax says. "Goddammit, Hawk. What the fuck are you thinking?" He runs his hands through his hair, looking furious.

But I'm furious too.

"Fuck you, Jaxon. I'm doing nothing wrong here. I love that girl."

Jaxon sneers. "You have no fucking clue what love means.

Honor needs time and space to heal. She doesn't need a man like you—"

"A man like me? What the hell is that supposed to mean?" I ask, pulling on my pants and grabbing my T-shirt.

"It means you don't exactly have a track record for taking care of people."

"Fuck that. All I ever do is take care of people. Why do you think I got in trouble time and time again? It's because I'm trying to take care of—"

Harper cuts me off again. "Taking care of people and using people are two different things. And besides, you can't exactly take care of Honor and her three children. You don't have a house for them. All you have is a truck. Do you have any idea what health insurance costs? A mortgage? Do you have any clue how much money it costs to feed three children? Diaper them?" Harper shakes her head. "Believe me, I know how hard it is."

"You want me to leave?" I ask them. Knowing that it's going to eat Honor up inside. It's going to fucking kill her. This is not what she needs right now. She needs comfort and security and the people who love her by her side.

"You need to go." Jaxon shakes his head, walking out of the room. Harper follows and I walk over to the bathroom door, knocking on it as softly as I can, turning the knob. But it's locked.

"Honor? Honor, baby, open up."

I hear her sob. But she doesn't open the door.

"I don't want to cause any problems," she says. "Please, Hawk. I can't ruin things for any more people."

"That's insane, Honor. I love you. Open the door."

"Just go," she says through muffled sobs. "Please."

I punch the wall, pushing my fist through the plaster, so fucking pissed. Honor won't open the door and Jaxon and Harper want me gone.

This is fucking insanity. My life finally seemed to finally be making sense, and then in one fell swoop, Jaxon and Harper think they can take it all away.

I cram my clothes in my duffel, lace up my boots, not even stopping to say anything to Jaxon and Harper on my way out.

Jaxon tries to stop me. "Listen—"

"Hell no," I tell him. With my knuckles bleeding and my heart racing, I don't trust myself to hold back from swinging more punches. "I'm not gonna listen to you. You have no idea what you're doing here."

I throw my bag in the bed of my truck and jump into the driver's seat.

Driving down the mountain, I'm full of rage.

I need to get my woman back.

And one way or another, I damn well will.

—

I decide to stay at the hotel in town. It's a piece of shit hotel. Well, it's actually a motel. I decide to stay in town because I can't drive away from the mountain. From Honor. I sure as hell can't show back up at Jaxon's place because I'm pretty damn sure he's gonna pull out a shotgun if I do.

But I can't leave.

I need Honor back.

I feel like shit leaving her that the way I did.

It's only been a day, though, and I can't very well show up at Jaxon's house and tell Honor to pack up the babies and follow me.

This motel is no place for a baby. For all four of those

angels. Timothy, Thomas, Titus, and Honor deserve a fucking palace. Not this shitty place.

I head over to the diner, starving, and trying not to get emotional over my memory of the last time I was here. How Honor and I drank our coffee and ate our cherry pie; how the whipped cream on her fork had tempted me.

It was where we started our torrid love affair.

The waitress points to a booth and walks over with a coffee pot and a menu.

She's the same waitress as before. Bright red lips, tiny waist, wide hips, the kind of girl who looks like she could be a 1950s-pinup girl. Her tits are pushed high, her hair wavy, and she smiles widely at me. And after the screaming last night I heard from Jaxon, I don't mind the friendly face right now.

And while she may be beautiful, she's not the kind of beauty that gets me hot. The beauty I love is the sort that Honor wears... understated and ingrained. Honor's beauty is timeless and forever. She is a summer breeze, and she floated into my life when I least expected it. She gave me purpose and gave me meaning. She is more than beauty, she is the proof of the power of love.

"Regular or decaf?" the waitress asks.

"Regular."

"I'm Josie, and you are? I saw you here about a month ago."

"Yeah, I'm Hawk. I've been staying on the mountain. Working for my cousin Jaxon's crew."

Josie nods, a hand on her hip, pouring the coffee. "Oh, yeah I know about the boys. Rosie, she's the one who owns this place—Buck's wife? Anyway, they were so good to me when I came into town a few months back. Gave me a job here and treat me like family." She smiles again. "So, what can I getcha?"

"I'd like scrambled eggs and bacon. Toast, too."

"Sounds good, sweetie," Josie says, winking. She turns away, just as the front door opens and Buck walks in.

"Morning, Boss," she says. "Just you today?"

"Just me, here to grab a cup coffee before I head to the job site." Buck looks over and sees me and nods in my direction. He calls out to Josie, "Actually, I'll have my regular breakfast. I'm gonna sit here with Hawk for a bit."

Josie nods before heading back to the kitchen.

Buck slides into the booth across from me.

My stomach is in knots. I can guess with one look at him, but he's already talked to Jaxon. Just what I fucking need to start my day.

"You're not gonna be at the job site today, then," Buck says slowly.

"Don't suppose I am."

Buck coughs, as if uncomfortable. "You know, Jaxon can be a little bit of an asshole. When I talked to him this morning, though, it's more than him just being stubborn. He's pretty fucking pissed."

"I don't doubt it," I say staring at my black coffee.

"So, what's the plan here?" Buck asks as Josie walks over, pouring his coffee.

After she walks away, I look up at him. "The plan? I have no fucking clue. I have a million things to do before I can get her back."

Buck raises a brow in surprise. "You want her back?"

"What the hell kind of question is that? Of course, I want her back."

Josie delivers our food, but suddenly I don't have an appetite.

"We're talking about Honor here? That's the girl you want back?" Buck asks, pouring hot sauce on his scrambled eggs.

"Who else would we be talking about? I love her. I love

her babies. I met her in this diner, sitting across from her and I knew. The moment I saw her, I knew that she was going to be my woman. I can't lose her because Jaxon and Harper think our love is wrong. I'll do anything to have them back. Jaxon didn't want to hear any of that. He just assumes—" I shake my head. I don't have the energy to fight with someone else.

"Damn, I had no idea you felt that way."

"Yeah, well it's our business. Nobody else's."

"I hear where you're coming from. Hell, I know that better than anybody else. I fell in love with Rosie right here in this diner, too. I know a thing or two about love at first sight. So, if you really love this girl, if you really want this girl, Hawk, you better make a few hard choices. It's time for you to step up and be a man."

"Right, I understand that. I just feel like there are a hundred things I need to do before I can claim her as mine."

"Starting with getting a house, I suppose?" he asks.

"Yeah, and a fucking job. Sounds like Jax took me off the crew. And the mechanic shop I used to work at, hardly gave me enough hours to take care of myself, let alone a family."

I shake my head, not really wanting to uproot Honor to some unknown city—Honor needs a support system, and if I go open a mechanic shop it's gonna take months to get it off the ground. We need a steady paycheck right now.

I look over at Buck, shaking my head. "You know, I thought the world was finally on my side. That all the cards were falling into place, but it was a fucking fantasy. Now I know exactly what I want, but have nothing to offer the woman I love."

"Man, I know you're bent out of shape, probably didn't sleep all night, but you need to get your act together. She doesn't love you because of your money, she doesn't love you because of your job. She loves you because of the man you are, the man you probably promised her you'll be."

I exhale, shaking my head. "I need to go back to the city then, find work there."

"Hell, don't let Jaxon push you around. You can get back on his crew, he just needs to know that whatever you are intending to do with Honor is pure."

"You think if I get my shit together, come back to Honor with something more to offer than my pickup truck, he might understand?"

"Hard to refuse a man willing to commit to a woman."

"I love this mountain. I love this work. I told you at the barbecue, how I thought I'd spend my life in a mechanic shop, but that was before I spent any time in the great outdoors."

Buck nods his head slowly. "You know, I'm co-owner in the business. You want to stay on the crew, you fucking can."

"Oh yeah. You think Jax will like that?"

"Jaxon doesn't have to know a thing about it. You've been working on the house out on old Mill Road? It's not done, right?"

"Yeah, there are just a few loose ends to tie up. They are bringing out appliances tomorrow. The whole thing can go on the market in about a week."

Buck nods slowly. "You need to buy yourself that fucking house."

I run my hands over my beard. "You're right, man. It's not much, but it would be a home. There are only two bedrooms, but that's enough space for us to start with."

"You think you could get together a down payment?" Buck asks.

"Yeah, I was thinking I oughta sell my truck anyway."

"If you need any help, I can always—"

I shake my head. "No, I have about 20 grand in the bank. I

was saving it to open my mechanic shop. I never thought of buying a house, I thought I was too young to settle down like that."

"But now?" Buck asks raising his eyebrows.

"Now I don't want to be fucking anywhere but here. Now I want to stake a claim for my family."

Buck grins as he brings his cup of coffee to his mouth. "Good. It looks like you've become a real mountain man. You know what's yours, and you know how to get it." He laughs, shaking his head. "And I'd be lying if I said pulling the wool over Jaxon's eyes for a few weeks wouldn't make me happy."

I laugh, which is a feat in and of itself. An hour ago, I didn't think I'd have anything to smile about for a long fucking time.

Buck claps his hands, getting down to business.

"Looks like you've got to get to work, son."

I nod, knowing I'm going to do everything I can, so when I see Honor next, I will be the man she needs.

onor

It's been five days. Five days of hearing nothing from Hawk.

I feel like a fool. I let myself believe he loved me.

Then he left the first chance he got.

Stop it, I tell myself. It's not fair to take this all out on him. What was he supposed to do? He's not exactly welcome here. He doesn't even have my number. And somewhere in the flurry of the last two weeks, I can't seem to remember where I put his.

I remember him giving it to me, scrawling his numbers on a piece of scrap paper after that first night together, parked outside the diner.

"Where are you going?" Harper asks as I load up a baby bag, buckling Titus in the infant car seat in her living room. "You keep leaving every day, and I don't know where you're going. You can't freeze me out forever."

I look at Harper, my mouth set in a firm line. I need to

figure out a way to get out of here. Soon. I don't have much money left—exactly $43. Enough for gas to get me back to the city a few more times.

"I've been making appointments with social services, just like you told me to."

"And? Are you getting very far?"

"No, I'm not." Titus is already fussing his car seat. "Anyway," I say, not meeting her eyes, "I gotta go."

I need to drive to another office where I'll sit in a crowded waiting room, waiting for someone to take me seriously.

But I'm a single mom with a bunch of children, and I'm not alone in needing help. Especially since I'm not answering the questions the government employees are required to ask.

Yesterday I sat in an office, finally being seen, and asked if there was any way I could get help for rent.

The woman was busy, and I don't blame her, I'm just one of the dozens of people she sees each day. Everyone needs something from her. Her hands are tied—it's not like she can just start writing checks to women in need.

"I'm just trying to get the facts straight, dear," she said, bringing her coffee to her lips. "Who is the father? And where were you living before you arrived at your cousin's? If you're in danger—"

"I'm not in danger. I just—"

How do I say don't want to tell you where I come from? How do I say I don't want to give you more information?

"I'm just trying to understand my options here," I tell her. "Is there job training or—"

"Sweetie, are you running from someone?" she asks.

I shook my head, not wanting to give up my story yet. Not without the permission of the other wives.

"I just want to know my options," I tell her.

"Well, you can fill out the form—the application for assistance."

I flip through it, overwhelmed with what I read. They need to know my Social Security number, my address, my medical history—all things that are stressing me out.

"It seems like a lot of paperwork." It's not the actual task that has me overwhelmed--it's the information they require me to give in order for me to receive help.

The woman looked at me blankly. "Honey, we need this information in order for you to get assistance."

"I understand. Is there a women's shelter, somewhere I could go..."?

"There is, but the shelter here doesn't have very many spaces. I could put you on a waiting list..."

I shook my head. Not ready to take that step. To give her my name.

"Thank you. I have a lot to think about." I stood, Timothy, Titus, and Thomas nestled close to me. Titus is in a sling and Timothy on my hip. I hold Thomas's hand as we walk out.

"You forgot the application," the lady said.

I turn back and take it from her hand, shoving it in my diaper bag.

I left Luke because I wanted a better life for myself... And I know what going down this route costs.

It's not that I'm scared of working hard. Pulling up my bootstraps and getting a job while scraping by.

No, I felt so overwhelmed about this because I realized what it will cost the rest of the people in Luke's congregation. This choice will cause them to lose theirs.

Harper looks at me again. "So, where are you going today?"

"I saw an ad online for a job. It's at a daycare and says you can bring your kids. So, I'm gonna go in and check it out."

"Really?" Harper asks. "That seems like a lot to manage, watching your kids plus someone else's."

"Yes, I realize that. But I don't have a lot of options if I want to leave Luke. And—" I want to tell her it wouldn't be so hard if she hadn't been so cruel to Hawk that night.

If she hadn't pushed him away, maybe he could have helped me sort all of this out.

Harper and Jaxon made it clear what they think about my choices. I can't stay here any longer.

"Listen, Honor," she says. "Things have been so tense this week. And Jaxon and I were only trying to do what was best for you."

I scoff, so irritated with her. "You have no idea what is best for me. You aren't me. Harper, I just don't understand how someone like you can judge me. After all you've been through." I shake my head, tears in my eyes. The boys are all strapped into their car seats and I don't want to make them wait much longer.

"You're not seeing things from my point of view," Harper says, reaching for my arm.

I pull away.

"I understand your point of view perfectly. You got everything you wanted."

"That doesn't mean I can't understand—"

"Yes, it does Harper. It means you don't understand at all. Things worked out perfectly for you, you got caught in a winter snowstorm and pounded on Jaxon's door. You fell into his arms and had his babies. You got your happily ever after. My life... it isn't happily ever after anything. And I thought... I thought I might get that with Hawk. But he left and I don't know if he is ever coming back. Now I'm alone. And you know what? I may not have any money, but I have a lot of love. And I still have hope. And even if it's going to be really hard—I can do this. I don't need you. I can do this all by myself."

I pull away from her, knowing the ticking clock on my life is picking up speed.

Time is running out.

I may talk a big talk, but I know I need to make a plan. Because otherwise, I'm going back to Luke.

Whatever I choose, I'm making this choice on my own.

– –

I have the application all filled out and ready to turn back in.

I'm applying for the job at the daycare, although the woman looked at me warily after I told her how many babies I would have with me.

"It might work, you just have to be willing to start really soon. Our other girl is leaving at the end of next week. You need to be reliable. You can't call in sick. Which means you have to keep your kids healthy too."

"And the pay?" I asked.

"It's 10 bucks an hour."

I swallowed. Ten bucks an hour, before taxes and social security. It leaves me with seven dollars and some change. Times 40 hours a week. Times four weeks... It would be so tight.

But I can make it work. With foods stamps and WIC. I just need to find a one-bedroom apartment that we can all squeeze into. That wouldn't be hard either, heck, we've been living in a one-bedroom for the last month.

But I know I can't have that life, even if I've sorted it all out in my head.

Because I'm sitting here in the bathroom. The kids are asleep. And my hands are shaking.

I can't turn in that application.

I can't take the job.

I know all of this because I must go back to Luke.

Because even before I take the test I know the reality of the situation.

I've been here three times before. My breasts are tender. I'm a week late.

I pee on the stick, wait 60 seconds.

See the positive sign.

Pregnant.

I can't take a job at a daycare knowing how horrible my morning sickness gets. There's no way I'd be able to care for my three kids, plus all the babies at the daycare, plus carrying a child.

I did this to myself. In the heat of the moment with Hawk, the condom broke, and after that, we didn't even bother.

All I thought about when I was with him was love. Pure unadulterated love.

But now? Now I feel like a fool.

I press my hand against my belly, tears streaking my face.

I don't regret for a moment being pregnant.

I have Hawk's baby within me, even if he doesn't want me, this is the most pure manifestation of love in the world.

There is only one thing I regret. And that is not opening the bathroom door the night he left.

CHAPTER 19

onor

Maybe if Hawk had come back for me. Maybe if he had fought harder.

Fought at all.

But it's been a week since he left. A week since my body was wrapped in his arms.

And maybe some people would think that one week is not a very long time, but my life has never been on the same trajectory as other people's.

I was promised to Luke young, had babies young, ran away from a monster young, and fell head over heels when I was young.

I've never had the luxury of living my life in slow motion. Every milestone has been accelerated. Which makes every day feel like a week and every week feel like a month and every month feel like a year.

My birth certificate may say that I'm twenty-two years

old, but I feel like an old soul.

And I'm trying to be brave.

I've been angry at Harper. She could make this easier on me. Jaxon could make things easier, too. But I'm trying to not hold these things against them; they helped me when I was in the biggest crisis of my life—until this latest one—and instead of wallowing in my reality, I'm trying to be brave.

Trying to be strong.

Thomas cries, tugging at me. "Mama, no," he bellows as I break down the Pack 'n Play. "Stay."

My phone rings, but I let it go to voicemail; I have too much to do right now.

"Baby, it's time to go, okay?" I kiss his little fist and watch as he goes back to his little race cars.

Harper walks into the guest room, shaking her head. "Where are you going now?"

"We're leaving."

She looks at me incredulously. "You can't go."

"You can't have it both ways, Harper. You can't be mad I'm leaving, but then tell me how I have to live under your roof. I have a family to take care of. I can't be living here knowing you're going to judge me."

I feel brave for the words I use, some people might think it's weak of me to go back to Luke's house, but I don't feel like that at all.

I left in the first place because I was trying to give my children a better life. And when he started calling two days ago, telling me my time had run out, that he was coming for his children, I made a new plan.

So, my plan is this: I'm going to go home to Luke, to my sister-wives. The children know that house, feel safe there, and I'll take the next three months before I start showing and try to save as much money as I can.

I'll convince Kind and True that they should leave, too. The three of us can go to social services together and ask for help. Luke doesn't give us access to bank accounts, but we get grocery money every week, and household expenditure money too. I think if we pull together we'll have enough money to leave.

And then we can involve CPS. Tell them why we had to go. Together.

I can't leave those women without any way of getting out. Together we can be strong.

The phone call went to voicemail and I pick up and listen to the message, ignoring Harper who is still standing in the doorway.

It's Luke. "I'm on my way to get you, Honor. I'm not messing around, it's time you return to your family."

I swallow, knowing this is the best option. For me. For my boys.

I pretend that my heart isn't broken over Hawk letting me go.

I walk past Harper and head to the living room. I secure Titus in a sling and Timothy and Thomas straggle behind me.

"So where exactly are you going?" Harper asks.

I swallow my bitterness toward her, but if she could've been a little bit more patient, a little bit more open, this wouldn't be happening right now.

Even as I think it, though, I know it's not fair to blame any of this on Harper. She's doing the best she can.

"Did you apply for another job or..." She bites her bottom lip, setting her baby in the swing.

"No, I'm not getting a job, I'm actually going home. Luke's on his way right now."

Harper's jaw drops. "No way, you can't go back to him." She shakes her head, tears in her eyes. "Jaxon and I were trying to do the right thing. And we've been trying to talk to you all week, but you shut us out. We understand you're angry that we told Hawk to leave, but he's no good for—"

"That's the problem, Harper. You're so scared of me getting hurt you don't even realize your choices are the ones that are hurting me. Hawk never hurt me. You did."

"I'm sorry, I'm just trying to protect you."

"By telling me who I can love?"

"You really think you love Hawk?" Harper looks incredulous.

"What happened to the Harper I used to know? The Harper who was willing to risk everything for the man she loved?" I ask. "I came here because I thought you were less judgmental than the people I go to church with. But Harper, you're so close-minded."

My words hit her in the gut, and she gasps, covering her mouth with her hand. "Oh, Honor, I'm so ashamed. You're right, it's not my place to tell you how to live your life." She wipes the tears on her cheeks. "Please forgive me, it was so wrong of me."

"I just don't understand why you dug your heels in so hard," I say.

"Honor you came here so you could be free, and I saw you with Hawk that night, and the only thing I could think was that you were going to be stuck with him forever. You were going to get yourself tied up in another man the same way you did with Luke."

I drop my head back. "But I wanted to be tied up with Hawk. And now he's gone and he hasn't called and... so I made my choice. Luke is coming for me."

"No, you can't go with him, stay here and we will call Haw—"

I step toward her resting my hand on her arm. "I don't want any more handouts. This isn't what I would've planned, but I'm going to carve a path for my own future. I hoped that future was with Hawk, but—"

"But now you're going to give your future to Luke?" Harper asks incredulously.

I shake my head. I explain to her my plan. How I'm going to convince Kind and True to go with me to CPS. I'm going to save money and get a job.

I'm not going to leave those two stuck with Luke.

"I just don't think you've thought this all through," Harper says.

I shake my head. "Harper, you're doing it again. You think you know what's best for me."

"I'm sorry. I know this isn't easy, and Jaxon and I have just made it harder."

"You can help by helping me load the van."

Harper covers her face, clearly shocked that I am determined to go through with this. Instead of arguing anymore, she simply nods her head and grabs a bag from my bedroom.

As she walks outside, I see that she's already pressed a phone to her ear. I can't make out what she's saying, but I can guess she's talking to Jaxon.

I keep loading up the van, with our clothes and the kids' toys, not quite sure when Luke will show up.

It's sooner than I expect. He pulls up and parks his car behind my van. He steps out, glaring at me.

I've still got Titus in the sling, and Timothy and Thomas are playing in the grass. When he sees them, he plasters a big smile on his face.

I know the only reason he wants me back is to save face. So, that the church believes that he has a perfect family like God destined for him.

"You all packed up?" he asks. "I didn't hear back from you after I called. You are supposed to return my calls, Honor."

"I've been busy. But the van is packed and ready to go," I say.

Luke steps closer to me and pulls me into an embrace. My back stiffens, my breath hot, my skin crawling with memories I want to forget.

In the month apart from him, I totally forgot how utterly horrible he is to be around. As I made my plans, I seemed to forget how terrible he makes me feel, how he pretends to be a saint when deep down I know he's a monster.

Harper walks out of the house, looks at him tightly. "Jaxon's on his way, Luke. He doesn't want you on his property," she tells him with fiery eyes. "So, don't try anything."

"Not gonna try anything, Honor's my wife. I can do with her how I please," he simpers.

"She's not your wife. This is not a legal marriage."

Just then, Jaxon's truck barrels down the driveway and he parks, jumping out of it before it even stops running, as if he can't bear the idea of Harper and me being here alone with Luke.

I admit that there is an echo of relief from seeing him here.

"She's not coming with you," Jaxon tells them.

"Oh yes, she is. Ask her yourself. Are you coming home with me, darlin'?" He wraps his arm around my waist. My entire body tenses, I close my eyes.

"Yes, I'm going home with Luke."

Harper shakes her head, "Jaxon, this is our fault. We got between her and Hawk."

Luke steps away from me glaring between the three of us. "Her and who?" he asks.

"No one," I tell him. "Nothing. Harper was just—"

Jaxon shakes his head at Harper as if willing her to stay quiet.

"What are you saying?" Luke asks. "Have you been whoring around?"

"Don't," I beg him, "the kids are right here."

"So, it's true. You've been a little slut while you've been away?"

Luke pulls back his shoulders, his face growing red; he's angry. "Now you'll have to repent, repent for your sins you little bitch."

I pull in a sharp breath, pressing my hands around Titus' ears, knowing he doesn't understand the words, but shame flooding me for them nonetheless.

"Do not call me that. Do not—"

I don't say anymore, because Luke reaches for me, grabs my wrists hard and pulls me to him. He squeezes me so tightly I'm scared my wrist is going to break.

"Let me go, Luke. "

Luke has never touched me like this before. Never gotten this cold.

But he's angry now.

"Who is Hawk? Who is this man who ruined you?"

"Let me go."

With my free hand, I shield Titus and I step away, but Luke reaches for my shoulder, squeezing tight, and pushing hard at me.

It all happens in a flash: Luke pushing me, Jaxon reaching for him, pulling him away, right as another car pulls into the driveway.

I fall to the ground, my arms wrapping around my baby, and my eyes close, barely registering that a man is running toward Luke.

I blink, seeing him punch Luke in the face. Luke falls to the ground with the single blow. The man stands over him, and Luke doesn't try to stand.

The children scream.

Harper cries. Titus sobs. My head spins and I will myself to focus on the reality of the scene before me.

The man protecting us from this monster is Hawk.

Hawk with his strong arms and his solid hands, keeping me from the man who hurt me.

Luke's face is bloodied, yet he still manages to snarl, "You're the man who turned my wife into a slut?"

Hawk drags him up by his shoulders, "You best get in your car, you motherfucker. And don't ever show up here again."

"You can't tell me what to do," Luke manages, wiping the blood from his face.

I'm sobbing, the boys are crying, huddling around me where I lie on the ground.

"I was only willing to come back because you never physically hurt me before," I shout, using the voice I'd been scared to use in the past. "But what kind of mother would I be to go back to you now? To take them back to a monster."

"I'm calling the police," Harper yells. "Your whole cult is going to burn to the ground."

"You're going to do that to Kind and True, your parents, where are they gonna go?" Luke asks, turning to me. "They'll be out on the street because of you."

"I don't know," I admit, not needing all the answers right now. I look at Hawk, knowing I have enough answers for this moment. "I don't have all the answers, but I do know this. You need to leave."

Hawk wraps his arms around me, helping me off the ground, kissing Titus on his head, helping soothe the boys. Timothy is already on his hip, Thomas, too.

"You're nothing but a filthy whore, you're not gonna take me down. As God as my witness—"

"As God is *my* witness, you'd better step down," Hawk growls. His voice is so firm and determined, all of us stand still. "You may think Honor was your woman, but you're wrong. She was never yours. You tried to take her, but she won't be claimed by a man like you."

I look at Hawk, my heart beating so fast, the afternoon changing so quickly. Hawk is here.

He came back.

I'm shaking, having felt so vulnerable in Luke's presence, but now I'm not scared at all. Because Hawk is here. His arms are around me and the boys, he is protecting us.

"To hell with you all!" Luke climbs into his car and drives away, screeching tires, as if he can't get away fast enough.

"Are you okay, baby?" he asks, cradling my face in his hands, the children between us.

"I am now. You came back for me. I thought you left forever." I start shaking again, hating that he ever left and trying to understand why.

"I didn't mean to scare you when I didn't come back. I was just getting my shit in order before I came to get the woman I loved."

I shake my head. "I don't need anything, I don't need anything put in order, all I need is you."

"Angel, I know you say that, but you have three babies, they need a place to sleep. A roof over their heads. A kitchen and a table. I needed you to know I could take care of my family."

I pull in a sharp intake of breath, "Your family?"

"Damn straight."

"Hawk, it's too much." I shake my head wondering why I'm getting everything I ever wanted when I made such a mess of everything already.

"Angel, I love you more than life itself. I never had a purpose until I met you. The moment I saw your face, I knew that my life was no longer my own, it was yours."

He's on bended knee now, looking up at me, taking my

hand in his. "Your boys are my boys as far as I'm concerned." Titus is still in the sling, and Thomas has his arms wrapped around my leg, and Timothy is crawling up onto Hawk's lap.

Jaxon and Harper watch us with mouths gaping open.

"I fell in love with you at first sight," Hawk tells me. "And I will love you for the rest of my life. Let me prove that to you as your husband. Do me the honor of becoming my wife." Hawk pulls out a ring, a simple gold band that holds more beauty than a ten-carat diamond. It holds the same simple beauty as our love—a never ending circle of unity.

"Yes, of course," I tell him.

He slips it on my finger, then he stands, wiping the tears from my face, pressing his forehead to mine, kissing me softly on the lips. My heart is overwhelmed, my body is shaking. Hawk is going to be my husband.

He loves me.

And he never left.

"I'm sorry I was gone for the last week, but I was finishing building our home. Signed the papers this morning, it's ours."

"A home of our own?" I furrow my brow, confused. "But how?"

"Sold my tools, a few cars I had back in the city. And I've been saving up to buy a mechanic shop of my own."

"You gave up everything for us?"

"No, Angel. I sold the stuff that held me back. It's time I got tied down to the only thing that matters. My family."

Hawk explains to Jaxon, Harper, and me that the house he was finishing up with Buck's crew is complete and ready for us to move in.

"Shit, you bought it outright?" Jax asks.

Hawk nods, explaining that he bought me a home.

"I'm so sorry, Hawk," Jax says. "I had no idea you were so committed. I should have never sent you away like I did. I thought—"

"I know what you thought. And Honor and I should've been more honest in the first place. Truth is, we feared losing what we found."

"Still, I could've done better. I shut you out."

"I could've done better too," Harper says. "I already apologized to Honor earlier, but let me apologize to you, too. I was so worried about protecting her that didn't realize I was hurting her." Harper pulls Hawk into a hug, and he lets her know all is forgiven.

"What I'm trying to understand is how you were out at that site all week finishing that house when I told Buck you were off our crew?"

Hawk smiles. "That's not my problem, boss."

He explains that Buck helped this past week, helping him figure out a home loan, and get the house furnished with Rosie's help.

"I even got you a new car, angel," he tells me. "That rusted out van won't do for my wife. Or my three sons."

I look past him and see a shiny bright minivan parked beside my old one.

I bite my bottom lip. "What is it?" he asks. "You don't like the color?"

It's a silver gray, sleek and beautiful. I can't believe he sold his precious truck for me.

"How many seats does it have?" I ask.

"It's either 6 or 7? Enough for the five of us."

I swallow. "Well, actually, it has to be enough for the six of us." I press my hand to my belly.

"Are you kidding me?" Hawk asks.

I shake my head. "I wouldn't lie to you."

"You're having my baby?"

I nod, seeing the tears in Hawk's eyes.

My heart bursts with joy, I'm so proud to be his woman, proud to be carrying his child. He falls to his knees, wraps his arms around my waist, Titus' little legs kicking him in the head.

Hawk kisses the tiny foot of Titus, then kisses my belly, before he stands and kisses me.

"I'm so glad you're pleased," I tell him.

He shakes his head, grinning. "Angel, you made a man out of me."

EPILOGUE 1

Epilogue 1

Hawk

When we go in for the 12-week ultrasound, it's just Honor and me. Josie from the diner has been our babysitter the last few weeks, and she came over today to help us out.

Of course, we're nervous and anxious, me more so than Honor. She's done this before.

For me, I couldn't be more excited to hear the heartbeat of my child.

We got married as soon as we could, we went to the courthouse and Jaxon and Harper were witnesses. They understood we couldn't wait. There was no reason to. Honor had never been legally married before so it was pretty straightforward.

The most straightforward part of it being my own unwavering commitment to her and her family.

In the van on the way to the appointment, she fills me in on the conversation she had this morning with her ex-sister-wives, True and Kind.

"They both have found a place to live. Luckily Kind has family in Washington state, and they came and got her and her children last week. She sounds good. Still pretty shook up, but that's expected."

"And True?" I asked.

"She has a brother who left the church a year ago, and he has an apartment in Boise. True and her little girl are there now. It's easier since she just has one child."

"Still hard. Damn, I'm so happy they had found a place to go." I look over at my wife, knowing how hard this is all been on her. She was under the impression no one was being physically hurt under Luke's hand, but it turns out he hadn't been as gentle with True or Kind as he been with her.

"Any word from your parents?" I ask.

"Not since that last letter." Honor licks her lips but she doesn't say more.

"I'm sorry, Angel."

She takes my hand, lacing her fingers through mine. "We're all grown-ups here, we all made our own choices. The shame is, most of what was happening at the church isn't necessarily illegal. But at least now social services are involved, they're gonna come check on families with young children again. And who knows if Harper's parents or mine are going to continue living that lifestyle, at least I know that True and Kind got out before they were hurt anymore." She shakes her head. "I just wish I could do more." She wipes her eyes.

"Oh, sweet angel." I pull her hand to my lips, kiss it.

"I know, I'm crying at the drop of a hat these days."

"That's okay, you can cry all you want, I just hate to see you hurting."

"It'll be good to hear the heartbeat." She smiles, through her tears.

"Do you think it's a boy or girl?" I ask.

"I honestly can't tell. But this pregnancy feels different. I'm already showing. Maybe it's because it's my fourth."

I squeeze her hand. "I'm sure everything is just fine."

– –

"The ultrasound technician presses his wand against Honor, and she grips my hand, staring at the screen anxiously.

"Is everything okay?" she asks. "I'm so nervous."

"Oh, you're carrying just fine, and I'm glad you came now and didn't wait any longer before your first appointment."

"We're pretty anxious to hear the heartbeat of our child."

At that, the ultrasound technician smiles. "Hear that?"

There's a *thump, thump, thump* and movement on the ultrasound screen.

"It sounds like two heartbeats," I say.

"Which one is mine, and which is the baby's?" Honor asks.

The ultrasound technician shakes his head, looking at her with a smile.

"Honor, that second heartbeat you're hearing isn't yours."

"What do you mean?" she asks, her eyebrows knitted together. She leans up on her elbows to get a better look at the ultrasound screen.

My eyes widen, I look over at her, seeing if she sees what I see.

"There are two babies here. Congratulations," the technician says. "You are having twins."

EPILOGUE 2

Epilogue 2

Honor

My back is killing me. My knees are killing me. My feet are killing me.

Basically, everything hurts.

I've done this three times before, I'm not exactly sure why it feels so excruciating now.

Oh, probably because there are two babies inside me this time.

"Baby, are you sure you don't want to call the doctor?" Hawk asks.

I shake my head. "I don't want to leave for the hospital until I really have to. And the contractions aren't that bad yet, besides, my water hasn't even broken."

"Well, I'm still calling Josie. It won't hurt to have her at the ready for when it's time to leave for the hospital."

I smile at Hawk's thoughtfulness and continue to waddle around our cabin.

Our house is more beautiful than I could've ever imagined. Probably because it isn't really a house all, it's a home through and through. We got through our first winter here, Hawk and I both getting used to the deep trenches of snow, being housebound for so many weeks. The boys loved it, of course, Timothy and Thomas would spend an hour getting bundled up just to play outside for ten minutes.

But the house would have a blazing fire and hot cocoa waiting for them when they returned with their father. Titus is too small to go outside, but I'd hold him on my hip, and we would look out and watch them from the window, my sons making snow angels next to their dad.

It was a picture-perfect winter, more beautiful than I ever thought I deserved.

But Hawk reminds me daily that I do deserve all this. And more.

And I'm beginning to believe it's true. Believe that we all deserve this kind of happiness.

That there is enough.

That happily ever afters aren't just for the virgins and innocents. A happily ever after belongs to every woman, no matter how complicated their past or present may be. No matter how many tears they've shed or how many battles they've lost.

I'm beginning to believe that every woman deserves a man who will fight for her.

Now it's March and the snow is melted, and the first tulips are beginning to bloom around the perimeter of our little cabin.

I walk out onto the front porch, resting my back against the railing, imagining what this place will be like in the summer. All five of our babies will be here, under our roof, in one place, feeling safe and secure, with two parents who love them more than life itself.

"Mama, potty," Thomas says, walking out to the porch where I'm getting fresh air.

I laugh. "You can go to the potty without me." I shake my head. Toilet training is not for the faint of heart.

I follow him to the bathroom, and while I wait for him to finish, I look toward the kitchen where Timothy and Titus are in highchairs, finishing a snack of goldfish crackers.

My life is simple and beautiful, and mine.

Hawk walks toward me from the kitchen, phone in hand. "Josie is on her way."

I shake my head at my worried mountain man. "It could still be days. Is she just gonna sleep on the couch until I going to labor?"

"I don't want to risk anything." Hawk kisses me softly on the lips. This husband of mine has been more neurotic than me this entire pregnancy.

The moment he heard we were having twins he became this bundle of energy. Assembling cribs months before they would be needed, researching the best car seats. And insisting that we replace all the boys' seats too, not just getting new ones for the twins.

I tell him we can't afford top-of-the-line anything, but then he puts in more hours at work, explaining that it's not about getting top-of-the-line, it's about getting the safest. And that sometimes the safest costs more money. But that he's not going to skimp on safety when it comes to his children.

I just smile and nod, inwardly beaming that he cares so much about his children.

I'm so distracted by Hawk's kissing that when he pulls back, telling Thomas to not pee on the floor, only then do I realize that's not Thomas peeing at all.

"Mommy peed on the floor, not me," he says, wide-eyed. "Mommy had an accident. But it's okay. It's just like Mommy says, accidents happen and that's okay."

Hawk looks at me wide-eyed, and I start laughing.

"Did your water break, baby?" he asks.

I look down at myself, feeling the shift already.

I nod.

"See, I wasn't being overly anxious. It's a good thing Josie is coming now."

Just then, I grip Hawk's arms, squeezing tight.

"Oh, my God," I moan. "Oh God, Hawk."

A contraction barrels through me, it's as if the moment my water broke my body went into high gear.

I shake my head. "Oh, my gosh, I think... Oh my gosh." My body sinks against the wall, and I lower myself to the ground.

"No, no, no," Hawk says. "Don't sit, we need to get you in the car."

"I can't move," I groan, another contraction twisting through me.

"Baby, you can't just sit here like this, we gotta get in the car. We have to get to the hospital."

"Oh, baby, I can't, I can't," I start screaming. Thomas looks at me, wide-eyed and I don't even care, my thighs are already trembling. I think I've dilated from 0 to 8 in 10 seconds flat.

"There's no time," I tell him, knowing we are way too far out in the sticks to get anywhere before these babies are born. "Call Harper and Rosie. Get them over here. Now." Hawk fumbles with his phone like a bumbling father-to-be, he is so adorably anxious— which is quite the contrast to me.

I'm a freaking freight train with broken brakes, headed to the station at top speed.

Hawk makes the calls and the whole time I'm screaming at the top of my lungs.

Minutes pass, next thing I know Hawk has me by the

shoulders, looking right in my eyes. "Angel, calm down, steady now, you got this, baby."

Sweat rolls down my face, how was it just a few minutes ago, I was looking out at our property getting a breath of fresh air, and now I'm on my back in my living room with contractions rolling through me one right after the other?

I focus on Hawk's eyes.

He tells me the boys are fine, that Josie is here. I nod, closing my eyes tightly as I brace myself for the pain.

The next time I open my eyes, he tells me that Harper, Rosie, and Stella are here as well.

Rosie brings me a washcloth and wipes my forehead, Harper and Stella have a sheet tucked underneath my rear, holding onto me as they help me breathe, in and out, in and out.

"You can do this now, you got this," Rosie says gently, and I believe her. I believe anything Rosie says right now, she had her twins at home, unexpectedly, too. If she can do this, I can do this too.

I push. I push again.

I'm not scared. I'm ready to find out if I have a baby boy or baby girl... Hawk and I decided to keep it a surprise.

"You got this, Angel," he tells me.

And I nod, believing him. I close my eyes and push.

I'm ready to meet our babies.

—

An hour later I'm in our bed, Hawk beside me, each of us holding one of our babies. The paramedics arrived after I gave birth, and it didn't take long for them to realize we had things under control.

Between all of us, we had delivered more children at home than those paramedics certainly had.

The babies were two weeks early, but they are healthy, happy. Beautiful.

Girls.

Two perfect daughters who I already know are going to be Daddy's Girls, through and through. Hawk looks like he has died and gone to heaven, his eyes glisten with tears, he wears a grin—he has everything he never knew he wanted.

"They're perfect," I say, my eyes glistening with tears. "Are we still going to give them names that mean love?" I ask.

My heart surges with pride as I look at my rugged mountain man. The man who gave me a home and a family and a forever.

He nods. "I think this one should be Ettie, and she should be Imogen."

I nod. "That's perfect. They were born out of love, after all."

Hawk brings my face toward his and cups my cheek with his palm. I breathe him in, accepting his strength and sinking into his courage. I'm so proud of my husband, how he's transformed from a man into both a husband and a father. How he never faltered in his commitment to us.

"I love you," I tell him, feeling weepy again. Thinking I might always be this way. I'm the luckiest woman in the world.

He kisses me and I know it's both a promise and a prayer.

"May we always be this happy," he whispers. "May we always see our children as a gift, our life as a blessing."

I lift my daughter to my breast, brimming with pride, nestled in a cocoon of commitment.

Knowing I found my happily-ever-after in the least expected way.

And knowing my mountain man will never leave my side.

CHAPTER 1
CHERISH

When we were four, I made him a mud pie and he told me I was as sweet as his mama's lemonade.

When we were seven, we sang in the choir together and he held my song book and I told him his voice was as clear and beautiful as a sunny day.

When we were ten, we pinky swore we'd be best friends forever and when he held my hand I vowed to never let it go.

When we were twelve, the Pastor told us we could no longer whisper in the back pew. That we could no longer practice duets for service unless an adult was with us. That we could no longer roam the woods alone, guitars in hand, and sit in our spot by the edge of the creek, singing until the sun set.

His hair was light, and mine was dark. His eyes shone, and mine were heavy. They always were, even when I was a little girl. But where I was hard, he was soft, and where I wavered, he always believed. When my mother died, he wiped away my tears and told me to hold on to hope.

That all was not lost.

He kissed me when we were fourteen even though they told us it was sinful—for my lips were supposed to be saved for my husband alone—but he didn't care. Not about rules, at least.

He said he only cared about me.

I believed him.

His kiss was the sort of kiss I could write songs about. And I did. We were poor, our families always on the verge of losing it all. Not that we had much to lose. Electricity and hot water were never guarantees.

But there was one thing that could never be taken from me, even if there was no extra money.

No one could take the journal I hid under my pillow each night.

And I wrote pages and pages of lyrics on his lips alone. One single kiss, under the shade of an old oak tree, the branches swaying in the September breeze, but my heart was sure and I wrote the song of my heart, binding it to my chest.

But when my father found the blasphemous words, he handed them to the Pastor, who burned them in front of all the other youths' eyes. We were the example, the dirty ones.

He told us to repent.

I cried.

He held my hand.

Everyone we grew up with in the church bore witness to this public humiliation.

He said he wasn't ashamed.

He said he loved me.

I told him I didn't love him back.

It was weak, I know--but I feared the wrath of my father. Of the pastor. Scared of them breaking me in ways that might never mend.

I can look back now and see that it was the final nail in the coffin, but back then we were still the Lord's Will Assembly, not the cult we became a few years later. He wasn't sent away—not then. Not yet. Instead, he was called a sinner like his older sister Harper. They made him make his wrongs right by constructing the church buildings. He would hammer nails into the wood until sweat dropped down his neck; until his hands bled.

It still wasn't enough.

The elders saw him as a marked man, though he was still a child.

I would see him working every time I entered the church... his eyes would find mine. And even though I was *just a girl,* I was no fool. I was a woman in enough ways. My body was alive, it had woken when he kissed me.

It would not go to sleep.

He loved me and I loved him and that should have been more than enough.

But it wasn't.

Because I was living in a world that was so small, so constricting, that I didn't know how to think on my own—how to stretch my wings, let alone soar.

Soon I was eighteen, and so was he. And he wanted me to run away with him, but I was scared.

"Let's go," he whispered, pleading with me. "Take my hand, and let me take you somewhere—"

I shook my head. I may have loved him, but we had no money, no car, and no education. My father told me daily where I would end up if I turned my back on God.

I may have been a woman... but I was a weak one.

He had been my lifeline when we were small—problem was, I'd never learned to swim. And suddenly I was drowning, I didn't think I could make it to shore.

If I'd been stronger, my story would have ended up differently.

His would have too.

But I wasn't. And when he asked me to go, I was too scared to follow. So, he stayed too. Refusing to leave without me, even if it meant he was at the mercy of elders who thought of him as a sinner, and of themselves as saints.

For three years he watched and waited, making sure I was okay. Three years of never turning his back on me. In stolen conversations, he would tell me that I was his and he was mine and that he'd never leave. He was patient and he was relentless. The church changed my name from Abigail to Cherish, and I was more lost than ever about who I really was.

He got stronger each day with the back breaking work they asked him to do, his muscles stretching the seams of his ironed church clothes. His chiseled jaw and tanned skin became more dominating with each task they gave him.

As he grew strong, I grew fragile. Though I'd never admit

that to him. I wanted him to believe I was as beautiful as I'd ever been. But I wasn't. So, I rarely left the house; I spent my days cooking and cleaning and helping homeschool my younger siblings, since our mother died years ago, and I needed to be here for them. My hair got long and my bones grew weary. I didn't want him to see me then... see what had become of me.

I was ashamed. I didn't deserve his heart anymore. He deserved a woman who was brave enough to leave when he had asked.

I was older now. Old enough to be married.

And my father promised me to a man.

A man older than my father. A man who already had three wives.

A man who would pay my father ten thousand dollars to take me off his hands.

The family needed the money. I looked at the faces of my four younger siblings, hungry and longing for more than they had.

I had let him down, but I wouldn't fail my family too.

I agreed.

Tomorrow I would be bound to a husband who paid for me, my sole job to give him children.

The man I loved could let the dream of me go.

I wasn't enough for him anymore.

And deep down I wondered if I ever had been.

No, that isn't true. I didn't wonder.

I knew.

He deserved the world, and by marrying a stranger, I could give him a future bigger than the one he had here.

CHAPTER 2
JAMES

The sun beats down on my back, feeling like this godforsaken garage will never get done. I look over at Jonah wiping the sweat off his brow.

"I'm exhausted," he says. "Ready for lunch?"

I nod, and the two of us climb down the ladder.

"I'm ready to call it a day," I tell him. "It's hot as sin out here." It's barely noon and already it's ninety-five degrees. Idaho summers are no joke.

"What's going on over there?" Jonah asks, pointing to a group of women gathered around the entrance to the church.

I frown, not having heard about an event at the church today. Not that I care for the bullshit religion practiced at the compound—but still, I usually know what is happening and where seeing as I do most of the grunt work to set up different events.

I head to the communal kitchen in the back of the church and see my cousin Honor there, a baby on her hip, her free hand mixing coleslaw.

"Hungry, James?" she asks. Her eyes are lowered, and I wish she'd meet mine, but she's become withdrawn over the last few years, ever since she was forced to marry Luke, the head pastor of this congregation—which is a fancy way of saying brainwashed followers.

Though I sure as hell would never use a word like that.

"What's going on out front?" I ask, grabbing a ham sandwich from a platter on the counter. Jonah follows suit, and Honor pours us glasses of ice cold water.

"There's a wedding tomorrow. The sister-wives are getting the place ready."

I frown. "Whose wedding?"

Honor twists her lips, her voice small, nearly a whisper. "It's Cherish."

The white bread is caught in my throat, and I cough, trying to dislodge her words. How did I not know this was happening? The only reason I've stayed here for so long is to make sure Cherish is safe. All I can think at this moment is that I've failed her again.

Jonah whistles low beside me.

"I'm sorry, James," Honor says.

"I've gotta go find her."

"They won't let you get near her," Jonah says. "Not today."

But my heart is already racing. I've asked her, too many times to count, to come with me. To leave this life behind. But she's always refused.

Now there is no more time. Now she's getting fucking married.

I can't let this happen.

I refuse.

"I have to go try. I have to convince her—"

Honor nods. "You should go to her, James. Maybe she'll feel differently now that the reality is setting in." Honor looks up at me, tears in her pale blue eyes. "I know I would have left if given an out the night before my wedding."

I run a hand through my hair, jaw clenched, wondering how I can get through her father's front door without him pulling out his shotgun. That bastard hates me something fierce.

All because of a kiss.

A perfect, holy kiss.

A kiss I'll never forget. A kiss I received when I was just a boy; a kiss that made me a man.

I grab another sandwich, eating as I walk to the door. Honor hands me a few cookies in a napkin. "Jonah, you'll cover for me?"

"Of course, man," he says. Jonah is a solid guy—though only eighteen. He's another part of the reason I can't just leave this place. I'm scared of what might happen to him

131

when the elders try their damnedest to tear him down. Being here ensures I can help him stand up again.

But if I can get Cherish to leave with me, I'll go in a heartbeat. She *is* my heartbeat. My everything.

Has been ever since we were little.

I gave her my heart and never looked back.

Out on the dusty road outside the church, I try to think it through. If she's at home, it's gonna be hella hard to get to her. Still, I head in that direction. If she is getting married tomorrow, I literally have nothing to lose.

When I pass Elder Luke, I drop my head. He is in the middle of a conversation and doesn't notice me. His house is in the center of the compound, and Honor's sister-wives are on their front porch with a bunch of little ones. The farther out on the compound I go, I pass a row of trailers and know I am getting close to Cherish's father's place.

Before the church became so fundamental, we were all living in town, in our own places, but once Luke came back with a vision of the future, everyone moved to this plot of land that he owned. My father was an associate pastor, so he got set up pretty nice—thank God too because I have a bunch of younger siblings.

Cherish's dad, though, wasn't as lucky—though the truth is, he's always been down on his luck. There has never been enough money to go around for Cherish's family... and without a mother to help, the weight of the family has been on her shoulders.

When I get to their trailer, I see her younger brother Abe out front.

"What do you want?" he asks. He's only eight but already looks like he's seen better days.

"Is Cherish around?" I ask.

"Who wants to know?"

I pull back, not expecting this. Then again, I haven't been

out here in a long time. Cherish turned me away so many times, I decided to wait her out for a while, not wanting to push her.

Now I wish I'd pushed her harder, faster. Stolen a van, taken all her siblings with me, got the hell out of this place.

"Just tell me where she is. Is she inside?"

He scowls, crossing his arms. A tougher sell than I expected.

I look down at my hands. "I'll give you a cookie."

He twists his lips. "Both of 'em," he barters.

I grin, liking his go-get-'em attitude. "Sure." I hand them over.

"She's at the creek. She's always at the creek when she's not here."

I nod in thanks, my chest constricting at the memories that well to the surface.

The creek.

Our creek.

Of course, she would be there.

I haven't been there in years.

"Thanks, little man," I tell him, already backing away from the trailer, snapping twigs as I run.

Needing to find her.

Needing to keep her.

Needing her to know she's always been mine.

CHAPTER 3
CHERISH

The sun beats down on my back, feeling like this godforsaken garage will never get done. I look over at Jonah wiping the sweat off his brow.

"I'm exhausted," he says. "Ready for lunch?"

133

I nod, and the two of us climb down the ladder.

"I'm ready to call it a day," I tell him. "It's hot as sin out here." It's barely noon and already it's ninety-five degrees. Idaho summers are no joke.

"What's going on over there?" Jonah asks, pointing to a group of women gathered around the entrance to the church.

I frown, not having heard about an event at the church today. Not that I care for the bullshit religion practiced at the compound—but still, I usually know what is happening and where seeing as I do most of the grunt work to set up different events.

I head to the communal kitchen in the back of the church and see my cousin Honor there, a baby on her hip, her free hand mixing coleslaw.

"Hungry, James?" she asks. Her eyes are lowered, and I wish she'd meet mine, but she's become withdrawn over the last few years, ever since she was forced to marry Luke, the head pastor of this congregation—which is a fancy way of saying brainwashed followers.

Though I sure as hell would never use a word like that.

"What's going on out front?" I ask, grabbing a ham sandwich from a platter on the counter. Jonah follows suit, and Honor pours us glasses of ice cold water.

"There's a wedding tomorrow. The sister-wives are getting the place ready."

I frown. "Whose wedding?"

Honor twists her lips, her voice small, nearly a whisper. "It's Cherish."

The white bread is caught in my throat, and I cough, trying to dislodge her words. How did I not know this was happening? The only reason I've stayed here for so long is to make sure Cherish is safe. All I can think at this moment is that I've failed her again.

Jonah whistles low beside me.

"I'm sorry, James," Honor says.

"I've gotta go find her."

"They won't let you get near her," Jonah says. "Not today."

But my heart is already racing. I've asked her, too many times to count, to come with me. To leave this life behind. But she's always refused.

Now there is no more time. Now she's getting fucking married.

I can't let this happen.

I refuse.

"I have to go try. I have to convince her—"

Honor nods. "You should go to her, James. Maybe she'll feel differently now that the reality is setting in." Honor looks up at me, tears in her pale blue eyes. "I know I would have left if given an out the night before my wedding."

I run a hand through my hair, jaw clenched, wondering how I can get through her father's front door without him pulling out his shotgun. That bastard hates me something fierce.

All because of a kiss.

A perfect, holy kiss.

A kiss I'll never forget. A kiss I received when I was just a boy; a kiss that made me a man.

I grab another sandwich, eating as I walk to the door. Honor hands me a few cookies in a napkin. "Jonah, you'll cover for me?"

"Of course, man," he says. Jonah is a solid guy—though only eighteen. He's another part of the reason I can't just leave this place. I'm scared of what might happen to him when the elders try their damnedest to tear him down. Being here ensures I can help him stand up again.

But if I can get Cherish to leave with me, I'll go in a heartbeat. She *is* my heartbeat. My everything.

Has been ever since we were little.

I gave her my heart and never looked back.

Out on the dusty road outside the church, I try to think it through. If she's at home, it's gonna be hella hard to get to her. Still, I head in that direction. If she is getting married tomorrow, I literally have nothing to lose.

When I pass Elder Luke, I drop my head. He is in the middle of a conversation and doesn't notice me. His house is in the center of the compound, and Honor's sister-wives are on their front porch with a bunch of little ones. The farther out on the compound I go, I pass a row of trailers and know I am getting close to Cherish's father's place.

Before the church became so fundamental, we were all living in town, in our own places, but once Luke came back with a vision of the future, everyone moved to this plot of land that he owned. My father was an associate pastor, so he got set up pretty nice—thank God too because I have a bunch of younger siblings.

Cherish's dad, though, wasn't as lucky—though the truth is, he's always been down on his luck. There has never been enough money to go around for Cherish's family... and without a mother to help, the weight of the family has been on her shoulders.

When I get to their trailer, I see her younger brother Abe out front.

"What do you want?" he asks. He's only eight but already looks like he's seen better days.

"Is Cherish around?" I ask.

"Who wants to know?"

I pull back, not expecting this. Then again, I haven't been out here in a long time. Cherish turned me away so many times, I decided to wait her out for a while, not wanting to push her.

Now I wish I'd pushed her harder, faster. Stolen a van, taken all her siblings with me, got the hell out of this place.

"Just tell me where she is. Is she inside?"

He scowls, crossing his arms. A tougher sell than I expected.

I look down at my hands. "I'll give you a cookie."

He twists his lips. "Both of 'em," he barters.

I grin, liking his go-get-'em attitude. "Sure." I hand them over.

"She's at the creek. She's always at the creek when she's not here.

I nod in thanks, my chest constricting at the memories that well to the surface.

The creek.

Our creek.

Of course, she would be there.

I haven't been there in years.

"Thanks, little man," I tell him, already backing away from the trailer, snapping twigs as I run.

Needing to find her.

Needing to keep her.

Needing her to know she's always been mine.

Want the rest? Download now! CHERISHED

The Mountain Man's Babies:

TIMBER
BUCKED
WILDER
HONORED
CHERISHED
BUILT

Los Angeles Bad Boys:

<u>COLD HARD CASH</u>

<u>HOLLYWOOD HOLDEN</u>

<u>SAINT JUDE</u>

<u>THE COMPLETE COLLECTION</u>

ABOUT THE AUTHOR

Frankie Love writes sexy stories about bad boys and mountain men. As a thirty-something mom to six who is ridiculously in love with her own bearded hottie, she believes in love-at-first-sight and happily-ever-afters. She also believes in the power of a quickie.

Find Frankie here:

www.frankielove.net
frankieloveromance@gmail.com

f

Made in the USA
Columbia, SC
20 May 2020

97944431R00088